To Crooked River

The Copper King's Daughter

To Laurence from Mama + Daddy

and Best Wishes from the Author

Dorothy Lawson McCall

The Ranch
December 1, 1972

The Copper King's Daughter

From Cape Cod to Crooked River

By

Dorothy Lawson McCall

With an Introduction by
Governor Tom Lawson McCall

BINFORDS & MORT, *Publishers*
2505 S. E. 11th Avenue Portland, Oregon 97242

The Copper King's Daughter:
From Cape Cod to Crooked River

LIBRARY OF CONGRESS CATALOG CARD NUMBER: 74-188836
ISBN: 0-8323-0203-1

Printed in the United States of America

FIRST EDITION

Introduction
By
Governor Tom Lawson McCall

Few children fully know or understand their parents, let alone their grandparents. But no history or anecdote is as fascinating or as interesting to a child as that which relates to his own historical past embodied in the experiences of his parents or grandparents.

Although aging somewhat, I'm still enough of a child to be fascinated with these stories of the life of my grandfather, Thomas W. Lawson of Boston—the "Copper King"—and my mother—the "Copper King's Daughter."

The fascination is deepened by memories of the years this youngster spent under his magic spell at the legendary Lawson estate, "Dreamwold," at Egypt, Massachusetts. It was the birthplace of my four brothers and sisters and myself—who found "Granddaddy" to be the most wondrous story-teller certainly ever to edify the tender minds of our generation.

Ill from a nearly mortal auto accident—and running close to the end of his gleaming personal era as a world figure—"Granddaddy" was still a commanding presence with an exceptional brain, when we knew him. And "Dreamwold"—all of it—was still essentially there, with its sweeping terraces and gardens, acres of handsome buildings, and the fleet of limousines that would bear us to private school at Hingham, complete with chauffeur and footman and "Granddaddy" spinning tales in the back to assorted grandchildren.

I think this book not only gives life to a great man but it portrays a time in New England and in the West that has been neglectfully overlooked in the histories and stories of America.

Tom McCall

Contents

The Copper King's Daughter

Good luck, always, Lawrence –
Gov. Tom McCall

1

Copper Is Where You Find It

"Can you shovel gold?" the banker asked the little boy.

Could I shovel gold? I nearly collapsed at the thought.

In a few moments, I was shoveling gold. That was forty-three years ago and I have been shoveling gold ever since.

Thus spoke Thomas W. Lawson, the Copper King, at the height of his career.

In the long period between the 1890s and today much has been written about my father, Thomas W. Lawson, of Boston. Anecdotes from his spectacular career still keep cropping up in newspapers and magazines.

In the 1890s Father was known as the "boy wonder," a millionaire at thirty and a thirty-times millionaire in the early 1900s. At that time, he was also called the Copper King. The name stemmed from a project he had conceived in 1897 which had as its object "the buying and selling of all the best copper-producing properties in America and Europe, and the educating of the world up to the great merits of these consolidated copper properties as safe and profitable investments." With two other men, Henry Rogers of Standard Oil and William Rockefeller, he organized the Amalgamated Copper Company, which offered $75,000,000 worth of stock to the public. In the resulting boom and later crash, manipulations in Wall Street resulted in Thomas W. Lawson losing millions, while certain insiders made millions. . . . But it all started, according to Father, in "those 'way-back beginning-life days. . . ."

"One day when I was twelve years old, I walked into Boston from Cambridge. I had my books under my arm, for I had started for school as usual. I had in my mind the practical necessity of helping to support the family. But I also had a powerful imagination already fascinated by the world of gold, which later in life made me a power on Wall Street.

"I had read the Aladdin tales of a mysterious world of gold, tales more marvelous to a boy's mind than those of the conquests of Caesar or Napoleon, or Jules Verne's *Twenty Thousand Leagues Under the Sea*—tales that told how one man with no other weapons than honesty, pluck, nerve, energy, and ambition might single-handed give battle to all the world, and win; and how, winning, he might command the power of kings to aid in making his country the greatest on earth.

"Enchanted with the marvels of Gold-Land, I had decided to peep at its mysteries.

"Standing at the head of State Street, looking down over the wharves into the harbor that, a hundred years before, had seen the historic dumping of the tea episode, is the old State House. On the ground floor, in the days of which I write, there was a big marine exchange, open to all, and running 'round the outside, a single wooden bench, hacked and initialed by jackknives.

"It was a four-mile walk from my home to that welcome-all bench, and with a grateful sigh, I dropped down among the old skippers who were airing themselves before returning to their craft.

"I had been but a minute on the bench when I saw beckoning to me from the banker's plate-glass window diagonally opposite—'Office Boy Wanted.' Ah, but Fate was a jolly fey, even in those 'way-back beginning-life days! My tired legs forgot their kinks, and in a jiffy I was standing, all of a tremble, before the opening in the mahogany and etched-glass counter, on the other side of which, only six feet away and in full range of my now bulging eyes, was a long bin heaped high with the shining Eagled- and Liberty-headed gold of my dreams.

"The coin was stacked in five-, ten-, and twenty-dollar heaps. A young man was shoveling, actually shoveling it—as if it had been the pebbles of the beach instead of the world's motive power—from the bins into brass scales.

"Every time the balance-pan tilted, a bell announced, '$5,000.' The shoveler would then pour the heap into a canvas bag, knot a string 'round its neck, and sealing it with red wax, toss it aside.

"I was so intent on the operation that I hardly heard the banker's voice, 'What can I do for you, little boy?'

"He smiled, for I was a little chap, and my spick-and-span striped linen waist and my strapped bundle of books spoke louder of mother's apron strings than of 'business.'

"But it only took us a few moments to consummate the greatest trade I have ever had hand in. I agreed to deliver my best services from half-past eight a.m. until half-past four p.m., six days in the week and in return, the house agreed to pay me three dollars a week. Oh, how big the amount sounded, and how I admired the banker for so nonchalantly rolling it off as if he was unaware of its ponderosity!

"He had evidently followed my startled eyes, for he asked, 'Can you shovel gold?' That was forty-three years ago. I have shoveled gold continuously ever since—no, not continuously. I was sent back to school the next day, and it was two days before conditions were pro-

Thomas W. Lawson,
destined to become the "Copper King."

Jeannie Goodwillie, his future wife.

"Father and Mother had grown up in the same neighborhood in Cambridge. They had gone to school together and eventually had fallen in love. . . ."

pitious and I again appeared at the banking house—this time with tears—to ask if my gold-shoveling job still awaited me.

"It was the following week before I could get away from school again, and then, at the end of a tearful confession, the banker put me in his carriage, and together we drove out home where he and Mother made a more business-like bargain than the one I had arranged under the lure of the 'Office Boy Wanted' sign. He would see that I had afternoon instruction and that I was made—a banker."

That was my father, Thomas W. Lawson, the Copper King.

Father and Mother had grown up in the same neighborhood in Cambridge. They had gone to school together and eventually had fallen in love. Their courtship was not a completely smooth one. My mother was a beautiful girl who, at seventeen, had had rheumatic fever. A picture taken of her at that time shows a wistful girl with large blue eyes and naturally curly blond hair. She had a dazzling smile and deep dimples. People were instantly attracted to her.

In contrast, Father has been described as a man "of piercing eye, bold manner, and fancy vest." This was the way the newspapers of the day saw him. He had a magnificent physique garbed in the wardrobe of a fashion plate. He was dark-haired, blue-eyed, heavy-browed, with a square jaw.

An enchanting girl like my mother, Jeannie Goodwillie, had other suitors. Besides Tom Lawson, there was another young man who was particularly favored. When my mother came home from Boston in the late afternoons, the two young men would be waiting on opposite corners as the trolley came into view.

As a rule Tom walked his best girl home. However, his rival was a persistent young man. So one evening Father delivered an ultimatum: "The next time I meet you at the corner, Jeannie, there will probably be two of us waiting as usual, Robert and myself. If you cross over to my corner, we'll walk home together and I'll take that as your answer. If you cross over to that other side, you'll never lay eyes on me again!"

Tom Lawson walked Jeannie home that evening and they were married soon after. The young husband established his bride in Winchester, after a short period in Cambridge with his sister, Mary, who became the beloved Auntie to all six of us Lawson children: Arnold, ten years older than I; Gladys, five years older; Marion, three years older; then Douglas, eighteen months later, and finally, eight years later, Jean. Before I was born, my mother had a recurrence of rheumatic fever, and I was practically born with rheumatism.

After the birth of Douglas, the decision was made that my mother should not have another child. However, seven years later she was pregnant. By this time

The Lawson children in Winchester, Massachusetts, home: Gladys, five; Marion, three; Arnold, ten; and Baby Dorothy in bassinet.

"The comfortable home in Winchester was the home of my childhood, the first home I remember, and always my favorite. . . ."

my father had become a force in the financial world. From Boston famous specialists and also trained nurses were summoned.

Doug and I hated the chaotic condition of our home at this time. It was no longer the comfortable, jolly place it had been. Mother was hidden away where we couldn't run to her and we were forbidden to see her. One overbearing nurse we particularly hated. I remember her grabbing little Douglas one morning when he had been particularly noisy and resentful of her invasion of our household. Baring his small bottom, she proceeded to spank him. This was too much for me. I crept up behind her and bit her on the wrist so hard I drew blood. Then Doug and I fled to our hideaway under the grand piano.

The morning my sister, Jean, came into the world, Doug and I were out in back of the house where we had a pen of rabbits. We had two Himalayan rabbits, a male and a female, with black noses and bright pink eyes. On this particular morning when we looked into the rabbit pen, we saw little furry balls rolling around. "Baby bunnies!" we screamed. Each of us grabbed one, and dashing into the house, we flew up the stairs. As we reached the top, a nurse snatched at us.

"Stop that noise, children! Don't you know your mother is very ill?"

Simultaneously Mother's door opened and my brother, Arnold, stepped out with a bundle in his arms. "Look!" we screamed at him, "little bunnies." Slowly Arnold lowered the bundle.

"Here, children, is another baby bunny. We have a baby sister." To this day, my sister, Jean, is known to all and sundry as Bunny.

2

"No candy for a year!"

Life in Winchester left me with some of my happiest childhood memories, for Mother and Father were gay, young people and we were the children in the big house.

Many early recollections are tied to the big, red house at 100 Main Street, but some are nebulous and undependable, as children's memories are apt to be. There is one which is impossible to place. I cannot say surely, "I was four years old" or "it was in 1891." Apparently it involved a recurrent experience because during the winters my parents, still young, probably around thirty, went coasting with friends on steep Bacon Street hill near our house. I always say of my mother that she was an invalid, due to the early attack of rheumatic fever, and another suffered about the time I was born. But during these years she was well enough to go coasting.

The group of young people coasted on double-runners and afterwards came rosy and laughing to our house. Invariably they gathered in the parlor around the grand piano. On it were two songbooks bound in leather. One was gray and contained Southern songs of the Civil War; the other was blue and in it were songs of the North. As they sang, the songs drifted up the stairs to where I lay cuddled in bed listening, and smelling the aroma of my father's cigar which blended with the music that floated up to my room. . . . I was the most secure child in the world.

Like all well-to-do, well-run houses of the period, ours had a routine that guided our days. The most important part of the morning involved getting Father off to work. While he and the rest of the family were having breakfast downstairs, a maid took Mother's breakfast up to her room. Shortly afterward, Mother held a meeting with the household staff. They would discuss the day's menus and plan what chores must be done. Soon we would hear Father's carriage clattering up to the front door. Immediately Doug and I would scuttle away from the breakfast table in time to see James Riley pull up the carriage. James would jump down, hand the reins to Father, and simultaneously, Father's partner, Mr. Allen Arnold, would appear, ready to step into the carriage for the daily trip to catch the 8:10 to Boston.

On the platform each morning was a small gathering of businessmen. Threading his way among them was

Joe, a freckle-faced, up-and-coming newsboy, highly popular with these men—Joseph P. Kennedy. The Kennedys and Lawsons were well known to each other as our home towns were adjacent. Another strong bond between the two families was John P. Feeney, one of the greatest of Massachusett's lawyers. Mr. Feeney, the lawyer, was a staunch friend to the Lawson family, for whenever trouble struck, he was on hand.

He was also a link between the Lawsons and my father's friend, Mayor J. F. Fitzgerald—"Honey Fitz." Mayor Fitzgerald was famous for his handling of large political gatherings, especially when they became excited or noisy. At the height of a fiery debate, Honey Fitz would leap to the platform and burst forth with the song, "Sweet Adeline." In that way, he soothed many a riotous meeting. The Mayor's beautiful daughter, Rose, later married Joseph P. Kennedy.

My father started his business career on State Street, Boston, and until he died, his headquarters were always there. Many times I heard him say, "When I come to the end, I would like cobblestones removed from State Street and my coffin placed beneath them."

As a young man, though, he had worked awhile for Standard Oil in New York and knew Wall Street well. Later, in Boston, he wrote his famous expose, *Frenzied Finance* (1905), an account of stock-market operations in Amalgamated Copper. At the turn of the century he controlled all the copper in the United States. Because of this he was called the "Copper King," well known around the world.

Many memories of this time do not really concern my older brother, Arnold, nor my older sisters Gladys and Marion, for they were at an age when they did not include a very young sister and brother in their activities. So, as one of the younger Lawson children, with most of my contemporaries gone now, and unable to contribute memoirs, I am forced to depend on a child's memory for facts about the family.

I remember certain glimpses—like the fact that Doug and I spent much of our time in the big, old-fashioned kitchen. At this stage in our lives we didn't care about the front of the house, but we loved Mattie Smith, the colored cook, and usually managed to be in the kitchen when she pulled cookies out of the oven. Then, the three of us would sit at the big kitchen table eating cookies and making paper dolls.

Faithful Auntie (Father's sister, Mary) was always nearby since she lived in Cambridge, and invariably was called in for emergencies. I was a child who always caught everything. Not so the rest of the family. They seemed to be invulnerable to disease; they were seldom sick. Gladys, for instance, was always greatly chagrined when Marion and I were absent from school for some kind of fever. She even went so far, when Marion was

The Copper King's sister, Mary, 1875.

"Mary . . . became the beloved Auntie to all six of us Lawson children."

coming down with one of her rare fevers, as to lie on top of her and breathe her breath.

When sickness struck one of us, Auntie was immediately summoned. She and the sick child would be isolated in the back hall in Arnold's room. Arnold would be put in the spare room.

The second floor of the Winchester house divided at the top of the stairs into a wide front hall leading to Mother's and Father's bedroom and into a narrow back hall leading to our bedrooms and to the attic stairway, which was enclosed. Also in this part of the second floor was a room lined with books and fitted with a desk. This was the library. There was also what would be called today the "guest room," but which we called the "spare room." This is where Arnold was banished when I came down with scarlet fever, which I'd caught from Marion. Of course Auntie had been called in to take care of me.

In those days, a sheet would be hung across the doorway of an isolation room and the sheet splashed with Platt's Chloride. One night when I was at the height of the fever, Auntie thought she smelled smoke. She opened the door and pulled the soaked sheet aside. The smell of smoke was strong. Gathering her nightgown around her, she pulled open the attic door and was greeted by a burst of flame. In a split second, she saw a hanging mop on fire. Grabbing the handle, she raced down the long hall and plunged the mop into the bathtub. Turning around, Auntie saw a small nightgown-clad figure standing silently behind her. Feverish as I was, barefooted I had followed her to the attic stairway and then down the hall to the bathroom. Oddly enough, I am still alive!

Another more pleasant glimpse of those childhood days in the Winchester home is of Father's carriage pulling up to the front door every evening. The next hour was a high spot in Doug's and my day. As Father stepped into the house we would run to meet him, each with one of Father's slippers in hand. When he was comfortably settled in his red-plush easy chair, we would pull up a little footstool, unlace his shoes, and put on his slippers. Now we were ready!

Father not only wrote poetry, he loved to read it and he could memorize anything written. Sitting in that comfortable red chair, he would take Doug on one knee and me on the other, and we would shiver in anticipation. For, in portentous tones, his voice rising and falling with the eerie story, he would recite *The Raven*, by Edgar Allan Poe. At the end of the poem, he would lower his voice dramatically and intone, "Quoth the Raven, 'Nevermore.'" With terrified shrieks, Doug and I would tumble off his lap and drop to the floor.

This same scene was enacted night after night. My gentle mother would say quietly to Father, "Now, you're not going to read that poem again tonight!" But every evening we two children would beg for it, promising we wouldn't be afraid—with the same results.

Another vivid glimpse concerns a fire and my father's red-plush chair. I know it was in the fall because, as I walked home, I scuffled my feet through leaves that had fallen from the trees.

It was dusk. I must have been late, for I ran up the steps of the side porch. Suddenly I stopped in horror. There before me was the sitting-room window, all ablaze. The kerosene lamp on the table beside Father's easy chair had flared up and set fire to a corner of the curtains. As I watched, the fire reached out toward the chair. I burst into the kitchen, screaming frantically, "The house is on fire! The house is on fire!"

In the kitchen all was serene; Mattie was getting dinner and the maids were helping, talking and laughing as usual. No one listened to the yelling child. The sitting room was on fire, yet I could hear conversation and laughter upstairs as the family waited for Pa to come home.

Then there was a sudden silence as the front door opened and Father's voice boomed through the house, "My God, where is everyone? The house is on fire!" I ran through the dining room into the hall and threw myself into his arms. Putting me aside, he picked up a heavy rug, threw it over the blaze, and smothered it.

Another early memory of my father involved a great commotion in the dead of night. It was late summer, still warm, and the family was visiting my Aunt Mary, who was then staying at Mount Desert, an island off the coast of Maine not far from Campobello.

That night all I could hear was people running up and down the stairs, doors opening and closing, and voices raised, "Pa must get to Boston! Pa must get to Boston!" Then more commotion, and a carriage clattered up to the front door. Then more voices—"President McKinley has been shot. Pa must get to the mainland tonight!"

Mount Desert Island was reached through Ellsworth, the last mainland stop on the rail line from Boston. That night, Father ordered a special train to meet the boat that carried him across Frenchman Bay from Mount Desert to Ellsworth.

Later the details were clearer to me. With the President's violent death, the bottom had dropped out of the stock market, and Father was needed in Boston to control a panic.

As a little girl in school, I tremendously admired my older sisters, Gladys and Marion. Sometimes, Marion—nearer my age—would take time out to play with me. These were high points in my life. Once, for some unknown reason, Marion decided to go on a year's diet. I remember looking at her with awe as she announced, "No candy for a year!"

My father's business instincts came to the fore. "Well,

Marion, if you are able to go without candy for one year, I will pay you five dollars."

In those days five dollars was a mighty sum to a child. Doug and I had allowances of twenty-five cents a week. We regarded Marion as a being apart. Five dollars! This gave me an idea.

I went to Father and said, "If I don't eat any candy for a year, Pa, will you give me five dollars?"

"Certainly, Dorothy. If you'll keep your word, I'll even give you the five dollars right now to put in your bank."

This was almost unbelievable. I agreed.

Next morning as Doug and I started to school, I saw two of my sisters' friends ahead of us and hurried to join them. I told them how important I had become with my father's business deal. They wouldn't believe me.

I said, "All right. I'll just bring that five dollars and show you."

That night the little bank was looted and I met the girls at the corner next morning, feeling very important. We started downtown.

One of my new friends asked, "Were you making up that story, Dorothy? Did your father really give you five dollars?"

Putting my hand in my coat pocket, I slowly pulled out the five-dollar bill.

"My goodness!" they exclaimed, "that'll buy a lot of candy."

Flattered, I broke the five-dollar bill and bought twenty-five cents' worth of candy. This was a whole week's allowance prior to my present affluence. From then on, my young life became a living lie. Every school-day morning, I would spend twenty-five cents for candy for my admiring friends and myself.

Every evening my father would say, "Do you think you will be able to last a year, Dorothy?"

And that little girl would lie and answer, "Oh, yes!"

Unbeknownst to me, my wise father knew that I was lying, so his evening query was a test. He was giving me a long rope to hang myself. He could not really believe he had a thief in the family.

Eventually came the day of reckoning. Money exhausted, once more I became just an unnoticed little girl on the way to school. I was forced to walk with my little brother again. Father, noting the change in my spirits, called me into the sitting room one evening.

He said, "Now, Dorothy, I thought I would check with you on your little bank. Would you please bring it down to me?" I crept upstairs and brought it down.

"Why, this bank is empty!" said the big businessman from Boston. "What have you done with the money, Dorothy?"

I was speechless. Father went on, "Do you understand that you have stolen from me; that you have become a thief; that the matter is out of my hands? I must call Chief of Police MacIntosh, and unless you can pay me back in a month, the Chief will put you in the town jail."

What was I to do? Mother was sympathetic, and since it was spring, she let Doug and me have some lemons so that we could set up a lemonade stand. We sold ice-cold lemonade for five cents a glass. By the end of the month we had $1.25, which I took, rather timidly, to my father.

Smilingly he accepted it, and patting me on the shoulder, he said, "I think you have learned your lesson, little girl."

Years later in answer to his question, "Why do you lie to me, Dorothy?" I was to say to Father, "Because you frighten me, Pa. When you frighten me, I lie to you."

3

The Gypsies of Cape Cod

While living in Winchester, most of our summers were spent at Duxbury on Cape Cod. At the beginning of the dog days—the hot, sticky weather characteristic of the East in July and August—Mother, with the help of Ada Cozy, our nursemaid, would gather her little troop, and bag and baggage, we would be driven to Boston by our man, James Riley. There we would board the South Shore train for Duxbury and the Miles Standish Hotel.

Duxbury was famous for its big, rambling, white-frame hotel, only a few miles from Plymouth. Many other New Englanders also spent their vacations there, including members of the Boston Symphony Orchestra.

We had wonderful concerts on the evenings when these great musicians played for us.

What happy days they were! I was part of a familiar group. I loved those summers at Duxbury much more than any summers in my later life. I can still smell the salt air and feel almost reunited with my summer friends of long ago. All of us—children, teenagers, and adults alike—looked forward eagerly to these vacations. Days were spent mostly on the beach. The Atlantic coast beaches along the South Shore were peppered with family groups. Children could play in the sand and run in and out of the warm water. Wooden bathhouses—six and eight on a platform—stood along the shore, and the beaches were bordered with sweetgrass and blueberry bushes.

After a rain at the beach, millions of tiny frogs—perhaps an inch in diameter—appeared, hopping on the sand. Doug and I and our friends used to collect them, keeping them in a large china chamberpot. Without our knowing it, one day we were moved out of our room, our things probably being put in with our mother's. This was the crowded season. We simply put the chamberpot under the bed in this room and promptly forgot about it. That night the new occupant of the room, a spinster, came flying down the hall, crying,

"Help! Help! There's somebody under my bed! He's got a gun!" Imagine her chagrin when the manager, hastily summoned, stooped over and pulled out the chamberpot filled with tiny frogs—all hopping wildly against its sides.

One of the principal attractions during our summer vacations at Duxbury was the trips we made with Mother on her namesake yacht, the 85-foot *My Gypsy.*

As a small child, Mother was nicknamed "Gyp," short for Gypsy. In the mid-1800s, Romany gypsies wandered freely throughout the countryside. Most people regarded them with suspicion, but not my grandmother. When gypsies arrived in Cambridge, they were always welcome at the Goodwillie house.

To these dark gypsies, my mother, then a child, was a little blonde doll. She herself was dazzled by them and saw no dirt or evil in them. Their life seemed very glamorous. One day after the gypsies had left, the little girl decided to start out for herself and find them. She thought this would be easy because the gypsies always disappeared in the same direction. She would head in that direction.

It was a long walk from the Cambridge house to Harvard Bridge. By the time she reached the bridge, tired legs were slowing down. While she was sitting on the curb to rest, an old gentleman noticed her.

"Little girl, where are you going? Is anybody with you?"

Little girl answered, "I am going to find the gypsies."

"Well, you look pretty tired to me. Suppose we take the trolley car and you can tell me where you live."

Through the years, my mother never forgot the kindly old gentleman who had come to her rescue on that hot summer afternoon. No trace of him was ever discovered after that.

The so-called king of the gypsies visited our family each Thanksgiving time. He was a tall man and always had his face bandaged. This was explained later after he had died of cancer. On those Thanksgiving days, he never failed to bring my mother a fine gift—and there was a special reason for this. Mother had never lost her fascination for gypsies and her treatment of them contrasted sharply with that of her neighbors. During the summertime, before gypsy women appeared, word went around, "Gypsies are coming. Better lock up your valuables."

Our neighbors closed their doors and took their children inside. Not so my mother. She would have Mattie Smith, our colored cook, prepare warm food at the large kitchen table, and the side door would be left ajar, to invite the gypsies in. Often several of the women carried small babies. These women would be taken straight up to Mother's room. She loved babies and would pick up a gypsy child no matter how grubby. Stripping off its dirty clothes, she would give them to a maid who would gingerly take them out and burn them. Then the baby would be bathed in Mother's own bath and dressed in our pretty baby clothes.

Mother's room was lovely. On the bureau were her diamond and emerald rings, pins, and other priceless jewelry, arranged on a large lace-edged pincushion. If a neighbor came in and saw gypsy women sitting on Mother's delicate couch or walking up and down the room carrying one of their babies, she would stop in horror and beckon Mother to come out into the hall.

"Why, Mrs. Lawson, take your jewelry and put it away. Don't you realize that you shouldn't leave your diamonds right on the bureau?"

With a little laugh, Mother would calmly answer, "Oh, I'm not worried about that!"

The yacht, *My Gypsy,* carried a crew of five and was seaworthy for long trips; she was equipped with two bunk bedrooms, a galley, and dining nook. However, because of Mother's health, trips were confined to short distances.

On those summer vacations Father would join us only on weekends, as business would keep him in Boston during the week. He would, as a rule, come by train and weekends would be spent with the family, fishing and sailing on the *Gypsy.*

My brother, Arnold, twenty years old at the time, had developed a marvelous singing voice. In fact, if it had not been for an incident at Duxbury, he could have made a career of that voice. . . . One afternoon, before Father appeared, Mother decided to take Doug and me for an afternoon on the yacht. With Ada carrying blankets and odds and ends, we set forth from the Hotel Standish pier where the launch waited.

It was a lovely afternoon—not a cloud in the sky. Arnold, down for the weekend, also decided to come with us, and suggested we go offshore for some deep-sea fishing. With fishing successfully under way, the ground swell suddenly proved too much for Mother, and the disappointed fishermen had to settle for a sailing trip nearer shore. In the meantime, unobserved by *Gypsy's* crew, a heavy bank of fog had been rolling in from the horizon.

Heading in what he thought was the right direction, the captain swung *Gypsy* around. In a matter of minutes, it seemed, boat and crew were completely lost in the fog. Were we drifting out to sea or were we still off the South Shore coast? It was then that Arnold, megaphone in hand, started shouting, "Duxbury, are you there?"

No answer came. Thicker and thicker fog muffled us. The captain ordered the bridge bell to start tolling, and it was then that we heard, in the distance, Father's answering shout, "Ahoy, *Gypsy*!"

As Arnold answered, Father's voice from the pier seemed one minute to be near but the next minute at a great distance.

For four hours, through the fog, the voices of Father and Arnold mingled in their desperate attempt to bring *Gypsy* in. On board, Doug and I, who had been put to bed, heard the incessant tolling of the ship's bell, followed by Arnold's voice, "Do you hear me, Pa?" Intermittently the answering shouts came, sometimes close, then seeming to drift far away.

Several times our nurse, Ada, came down to check on Doug and me. "Children, children, why aren't you asleep?"

"But, Ada, we're scared to death. Are we going to drown, or drift out to sea?"

"Nonsense, children, go to sleep." Looking at Ada, we saw a change in her smooth, ebony-colored skin. It had taken on a strange, grayish hue, and we realized she herself was scared to death.

Back at Duxbury on the pier, friends were gathering around Father; suggestions were coming from all sides. In the midst of this turmoil, a figure came running down from the hotel. It was Ed Brown, a close friend of the family from Springfield, Massachusetts. Grabbing Father by the arm, he spoke quietly, "Now, Mr. Lawson, hold everything. I have an idea! The last call from *Gypsy* came from the direction of Plymouth. In a matter of hours, daylight will be here."

"I'll leave you here and run along the beach toward Plymouth. Every few minutes, I'll shout to *Gypsy* to come along."

Looking at him with gratitude, Father said, "God bless you, Ed. You're a real friend."

Turning away from Father, Mr. Brown started on his epic trip. The last thing people heard was his call growing fainter and fainter, "*Gypsy*, where are you? Arnold, do you hear me?" There was only silence from the ocean and silence from the shore.

At the first faint tinge of dawn, the voice of the faithful friend from Springfield led the little fog-drenched pleasure yacht, *My Gypsy*, into Plymouth Harbor. Mr. Brown's persistent calls from shore, moving ever toward Plymouth, had brought the family out of the fog and the threatening deep sea into the safety of Plymouth Harbor. . . . But, after that night of calling back and forth through the fog, Arnold's singing voice was never the same again.

One of the outstanding entertainments on these fishing trips was the deep-sea fishing competition, which usually took place on weekends. Everyone on board, including the crew, was invited to join in the afternoon contest (fishing for cod and haddock). Father always offered a one-dollar bill for the first fish, a one-dollar bill for the largest fish, and a one-dollar bill for the most fish.

One of these expeditions stands out starkly in my memory. It so chanced that Doug and I were left alone on deck after the grownups had gone into the dining room for lunch. We decided to try our fishing luck in a "clear field." We dropped our lines overboard and waited. Suddenly Doug screamed,

"Help me, Dote! Help me!" As I turned to look at him, I realized the fish on the end of that line was going to be too much for Doug. His feet were braced, he was breathing hard, and his blue eyes were fairly popping.

"Help me, Dote! I can't hold on much longer."

By this time, Doug was just barely hanging on to the line. Turning toward the dining room, I screamed, "Help, Pa, help! Doug is being pulled overboard! Doug is being pulled overboard!" In answer to my frenzied cries, Father dashed from the dining room, followed by the guests. Grabbing Doug with one hand, he clenched his fist around the heavy fish line and together they hung on until the crew came to the rescue. One of the crew reeled in Doug's line–his catch was a 24-pound haddock!

When the large fish was finally subdued and gaffed, a very excited Doug watched his prize catch hung up on the aft deck for everyone to see.

4

"I began to feel my oats."

As Father's influence increased in the business world it seemed wiser for him to be nearer his Boston office.

Leaving the friendly surroundings in Winchester for Beacon Street, Boston, was like moving to an entirely different country. The whole way of life was foreign, particularly to us children. My mother knew that the move would be a sacrifice for the family, but her sensible Scotch wisdom understood that Father would be better off in Boston. Mother may have understood the necessity of the move, but the younger Lawson children objected loudly. On the other hand, my two older sisters, Gladys and Marion, and older brother, Arnold, were enthusiastic about the new life that they could envision.

In contrast to the easy comfort and friendly servants at the Winchester house, when we moved to 1 Charlesgate East in Boston, we were confronted by an Italian chef in formal chef's clothes, a kitchen maid, butler, waitress, chambermaid, and most important of all, a German housekeeper, Miss Behmer. Miss Behmer was elderly, carried a bunch of keys at her waist, and wore a wig, parted stiffly and done in crinkles. Underneath it we could see her pink scalp. She was extremely dictatorial and in complete charge of the household staff. In addition, there was Bunny's nurse, Lizzie Welch, well known as "Dowager Queen of the nurses on Commonwealth Avenue." Mother had her own maid.

We moved to Boston in the early fall of 1898 and as Christmas drew near, Doug and I complained bitterly because we had to have Christmas in the new house. That year, Christmas came on Sunday, but would be observed on Monday. Mother made up her mind to take us over to the beloved Winchester house for a pre-Christmas. She arranged to have Amelia, our Winchester housekeeper, open up the old house. It was a welcome sight when the three of us stepped from the carriage on that Christmas weekend.

While we children were playing happily with our friends, Mother sent Amelia to Woburn to buy presents for our Christmas stockings. That night Mother and Amelia had a wonderful time filling the stockings. Next morning, there was wild excitement as we emptied those stockings, for they were stuffed with all sorts of gifts from the 5- and 10-cent store. There were tops, doll furniture, marbles in a bag, and the like, and in the toe of each stocking was a shiny quarter. That evening, we drove back to the Boston house for a million-dollar Christmas.

It has always been hard for outsiders to break into a new society, especially in stony-faced Boston, but there is one shortcut—horses. If a person knows his horses, it is very easy to break into almost any society.

In looking over an old magazine article I came upon the following sentence, "Neither Mr. or Mrs. Lawson care for society and they are rarely seen at functions, except at the Boston or New York horse show." This brings to mind a rather amusing episode.

Our box at the Boston horse show was always beside the runway where the horses and carriages came into the ring. I don't think any automobile or airplane will ever have the glamor of those sleek, shining horses with their jangling bits froth-spattered as, with stamping hoofs, they swept into the ring.

My father's first pair of show horses were aptly called "Gorgeous" and "Glorious." From then on all his blue-ribbon winners bore either "Gorgeous" or "Glorious" as a prefix to their names.

The first time our little sister, Bunny, came with the family to the Boston horse show, she was only four or five years old and especially excited as "Papa" was showing one of his trotting horses. The horse in question, a chestnut trotting mare named Baronness, was all fire and no sense. However, she came quietly into the ring with Father handling the lines.

Suddenly the band struck up. Baronness rose straight in the air on her hind legs, and plunging downward, pulled Father from the sulky. Before startled attendants could stop the runaway, Father was dragged several times around the ring, facedown in the tanbark. However, to my small sister, Bunny, it was a great circus show. With high-pitched squeals of glee she shrieked, "Do it again, Papa! Do it again!"

Horses were an integral part of life for the Lawson family. When Father later developed the Dreamwold estate on the south shore of Cape Cod, he was fulfilling a dream—to own a glorified farm on which he could raise the best animals of all kinds, particularly a horse of a typical American breed. Many famous horses were cared for in the great stables on the thousand acres of Dreamwold.

From the time the Lawson children walked, they rode. The whole family was "horse-minded." Even the little girls, in pants, rode astride their ponies. Of course, when the girls became young ladies they graduated to sidesaddle riding habits.

One scene—very vivid in my mind even today—is the night our cream-colored Shetland pony, Missy, gave

Sister, Bunny, on pony at Dreamwold.

"From the time the Lawson children walked, they rode. The whole family was 'horse-minded.' Even the little girls, in pants, rode astride their ponies. Of course, when the girls became young ladies they graduated to sidesaddle riding habits."

birth to a cream-colored colt, promptly named Sissy. Father brought the little horse into the house in his arms. Looking like a baby lamb, Sissy stood wobbling on the shiny dining-room table. As Sissy grew, we drove the two Shetlands as a pair, hitching them to a basket wagon full of miscellaneous children. Our trips were frequently to the neighboring bakery. Our chief errand there was the purchase of half a dozen big, round sugar cookies, which we fed to those cream-colored Shetlands.

Father's interest in horses had some exciting results. He was always investing in spirited saddle horses for himself. One of his investments was a jet-black horse called Kentucky—a "runaway." "Kentuck" was a challenge for Father. When James Riley, the coachman, brought him around one morning, Father was waiting impatiently, anxious to get into the saddle. Doug and I were on the sidewalk watching when, like a jet-black streak, "Kentuck" shot across the street and on up past Madam Herrick's mansion. That little English lady was on her porch and as she explained later,

"When that handsome young Mr. Lawson went by here on that black devil, he was going like Jehu!"

After Father had been rescued and doctors summoned, Doug and I tiptoed to the door of the bedroom. There lay a figure in the bed, bandaged from head to toe like a mummy. We ran screaming away, "Oh, that's not Pa! That's not Pa!"

Later in life Father philosophized, "The more horses you ride, the more trips you take, the more seas you sail, the more chances you take, the more you expose yourself to danger." But Father had incredible luck, and it seemed to include the whole family. This fact was brought out many times; for instance, take the story of the subway explosion in Boston:

While we still lived in Winchester, Gladys and Marion had been placed in Miss Gilman's School, a fine private school on Commonwealth Avenue; they were day scholars and commuted by train. At the station in Boston they were met daily by Father's cab driver, Dennis MacIntyre. Dennis was always on hand to take Father back and forth to the train on his way to the office. The same arrangement was made for my sisters.

About this time, one of the great New England tragedies took place. Metropolitan Boston, with its narrow streets, was beginning to suffer from an expanding traffic jam. Something had to be done. The city fathers finally decided a subway was the only answer. Construction followed immediately. One afternoon as the cab driver was on his way to Miss Gilman's School to pick up the girls, a tremendous explosion took place at the subway on Fremont Street. The resulting carnage was beyond belief. The explosion had occurred at the height of the shopping hour, killing and injuring an untold number of shoppers. One of the fatalities was Dennis MacIntyre, along with his horse and his cab.

Had the cab been on its return trip, my two sisters, Gladys and Marion, would also have been blown to bits.

My sister, Marion, a great rider, was the only one who rode to the hunt, and she was one of the first young women to ride cross-saddle in Boston. She bought the first cross-saddle suit from London. The coat was modeled after a man's hunting coat; underneath was a pair of riding breeches. On each knee of the breeches was a button; the lower part of the coat fastened to that button, and the Lawson girls were never allowed to ride without the coat fastened—and they were never permitted to ride cross-saddle in the Boston park, even with the proper buttoning.

There was always a group of friends riding with us on the family horses, and this led Father to take some necessary action. After making a speech in Kansas City, he came across a breed of horse he had never seen before. This was the Western "fuzz tail," the size of a Polo pony. He brought ten of these animals back from that trip, fitted out with western saddles.

The day the horses arrived, we were all at the stables to see them. While we were inspecting the ponies, Father said, "The reason I have bought these ponies is to protect my fine show horses. You all have a habit of putting unskilled riders, your friends and mine, on some of my best stock. Poor riders, in the long run, are very bad for good horses."

In all the years I never remember his buying a really quiet horse. Runaways were part of everyday living from our childhood on. I've often been told about one summer day at Duxbury on Cape Cod when Father was driving a new horse. Because the animal had seemed quiet he decided to take me, his little daughter, Dorothy, along. While being driven along the edge of the beach, the new horse suddenly shied at a gigantic horseshoe crab. He reared, took the bit in his teeth, and bolted. Father, realizing the danger, threw one arm about me and with the other guided the carriage toward the road. Undaunted, the black horse raced on—Father's hands on the lines having little or no effect. Sensing oncoming peril in the situation, Father made a quick decision. Lifting me from the seat beside him, he tossed me as lightly as possible onto a blueberry bush. That was my first runaway experience.

The second runaway I remember was one sunny morning when our horse Rex bolted down Main Street with little Doug and me pinned in the back seat. . . . Sometimes Doug and I were permitted to drive to the station with Father on his way to the Boston office. James Riley, the coachman, would bring Rex and the carriage to the curb in front of the house, step down, hand the reins to Father, then join us in the back seat where we eagerly waited.

On this particular morning, as James held the lines out to Father, they fell short and dropped on the pavement. Rex, frightened by the falling lines, swerved and reared, hitting his nose on the nearby telephone pole. With a terrified jump, he headed down the street. Italians working on the road threw down their picks and shovels and ran, waving and screaming, after the fleeing carriage—in the back seat of which two small children were holding out their arms, calling "Help! Help!" This was the last Father saw of us because the street turned there and the carriage careened around the corner toward the center of town. To add to his horror, at the same time came a warning blast from the Montreal Express on its daily trip through Winchester to Boston.

As Father stood transfixed on the sidewalk, a friend, Miss Gertrude Tyler, came driving leisurely by in her phaeton. Seeing him there, she drew up, calling,

"Mr. Lawson! Mr. Lawson! What has happened?" Without even answering, Father leaped in beside her.

"Race, Gertrude, race! Rex has run away and the children are in the carriage."

Meanwhile, at the center of town at the railroad crossing, horrified bystanders covered their eyes as the runaway horse and children swung into view. The gates were down and a second blast from the approaching train served notice that the express would thunder by at any minute. Realizing the imminent danger, the gateman, with lightning-like perception, slowly raised the gates just high enough to clear the terrified horse and children. Through the partially raised gates, Rex shot, coming to a dead stop across the street from Winn and Kelly's Livery Stable.

Within seconds, the Montreal Express thundered through on its way to Boston. As the gateman raised the gates again, the horse and carriage with Father and Gertrude Tyler plunged across the tracks. Speechless with emotion, Father rushed to embrace his two waiting children.

The wildest runaway horse incident occurred on a spring afternoon when we lived in the Boston house. Both of my older sisters were away at the time. From our arrival in Boston, Doug and I had taken riding lessons from a wonderful Scotch riding master, Charlie Steele. We were placed in a class with other children our own age. With all our riding in Winchester, I never realized there could be so much red tape in riding a horse. The oft-repeated and much-hated word which we heard over and over was, "Form, form, Miss Dorothy; form, Mr. Douglas." In these lessons, we would ride out onto the bridle path in the park. We used Steele's horses—all except one called Harpoon, a hunter which Mr. Steele himself rode. The others were poky, quiet horses. Now while my sisters were away and I was the oldest Lawson girl at home, I began to feel my oats. I said to Father,

"With our Newbury Street stables full of blue-ribbon horses, why do I have to go on riding Steele's old plugs?"

Father took me up on this and consulted with our head coachman, Michael Kelly. Since my sisters had left, there had been a new addition to the stables, a chestnut named Glorious Radi, scarcely ever beaten in a show ring. Radi had been exercised daily in the park by grooms, though even Michael had never ridden him. Because the grooms had had no trouble with him, Michael said, "Let Miss Dote ride Radi. I'll send one of the grooms over with him. After all she's going to ride with Steele."

For the event, our new maid—a light-skinned Negress named Sarah—came out to the backyard to take a picture of me in my riding clothes. Right away she said she was afraid to see me ride that horse and told a gruesome story of a family she had worked for. "A young girl, Miss Dorothy, about your age, wanted to ride one of her father's horses. Her family tried to talk her out of it. I've never forgotten it; when she leaped into the saddle the horse went right over backwards. I'll never forget how she looked. There lay that lovely young woman, her riding clothes torn and bloody. I'll never forget it."

I hurried away from the yard to the sidewalk where the English groom, Walter Swan, waited with handsome Radi, Steele beside him on Harpoon. With Sarah's story vivid in my mind, Radi looked like too much to handle. Walter put his hand under my foot and helped me up. I clutched the reins and settled lightly into the saddle.

Walter took his hand off the bridle, and with a snort of defiance the horse reared. The groom called to me,

"Give him his head, give him his head, Miss Dote, or he'll rear over backwards!" Behind me I heard Steele, the riding master shout,

"Sit tight, Miss Dorothy, and pull!" I loosened the reins and cried, "Whoa, Radi!" as I sawed and pulled on the bit. With all my might and main I pulled, but the horse's head was down and I pulled on a stone wall.

On dashed Radi, unbeaten in any show ring, and now fighting mad. He had reared at the curb, the first touch of my hand on the bridle signaling here was something to be got rid of.

"Give him his head, Miss Dote," Walter, the groom, had warned, "or he'll rear over backwards!"

Why had I wanted to ride this creature? Why hadn't anyone stopped me? Questions tumbled through my brain—but there was only one answer—Miss Dorothy usually had her own way!

Behind me, that spring afternoon, beside Walter, the groom, stood my horrified Father, rooted to the spot. Steele, the riding master, seeing the futility of chase, checked his mount and waited. He must have sent up a prayer to Heaven; he would not see his prize pupil dashed to pieces.

On, on we raced, out of the narrow side street and into the busy cross-section where the avenue leads into the park. Way over in the distance, against the skyline, a train puffed slowly across the bridge. I remember how lazily the smoke rose in the blue.

"I am going to be killed," I thought. "I, Dorothy Lawson, am going to be dashed to pieces and be dead forever. Tomorrow's papers will tell of my mangled flesh and bones messed up all over the sunny street. In a second, it will happen."

I closed my eyes and tried to scream. A guttural noise rasped in my throat and I opened my eyes. We had cleared the intersection and were shooting by the Somerset Hotel.

"Whoa, Radi—whoa, boy—steady now!" Feebly my voice rose as I remembered Steele's advice, "Talk to your horse, Miss Dorothy—always talk to your horse." And, as before, I sawed and pulled on the futile bit.

Around the corner, behind the Somerset Hotel, came a leisure carriage—old ladies out for an airing. Sleepy horses jogged peacefully to the occasional cluck of a sleepy old coachman.

Now it would happen! It was no use . . . there was no time, no strength left to shriek a warning. We would all be strewn over the street—old ladies, horses, carriage, coachman, me.

I leaned back, back—and gave a final supreme pull. It meant the curb, but no old ladies, and either way I was done for. With a sickening sound, Radi went down on his knees on the curb. The carriage with the old ladies jogged by to safety.

Frenzied now beyond any control, the horse came to his feet. I found myself still in the saddle–then Radi was off again, both knees bleeding. Half a block ahead lay Massachusetts Avenue teeming with traffic. Between that busy street and us, I saw only two moving objects.

"Oh, stop him!" I called, sobbing wildly, "Stop him!"

Afterwards I realized that a groom from Bradley's Livery Stable threw the riderless horse he was leading straight into Radi's path. This broke the chestnut's furious pace. All I knew at the time was that a horse was galloping by.

One more object moved on the quiet, almost-deserted side street, a diminutive groom riding a horse from the local stable.

"Oh, do stop him!" Tears rained down my face, the cry a pitiful wail–"Stop him, stop him!"

The anguished cry, a terrified child, and a wild, bleeding horse meant only one thing to that little Irish groom –a runaway must be stopped! He slipped from his saddle and stood resolutely in the path of Glorious Radi.

The maddened animal swerved slightly to miss the obstacle. The groom–his name was Joe Beale–swung onto the bridle and hung on.

Just this side of Massachusetts Avenue, Radi slowed down, then came to a panting, quivering standstill, the little Irishman dragging heavily on the bridle.

Marion on Sport—a fiery, golden sorrel—at Dreamwold's main gate; small railway station of Egypt shows at right.

"My sister, Marion, a great rider, was the only one who rode to the hunt, and she was one of the first young women to ride cross-saddle in Boston."

From nowhere a crowd gathered around us, and a white-faced riding master galloped up to me with, "Great riding, Miss Dorothy!" Even now I remember my shaky answer,

"Riding? I guess I was praying." Then my father lifted me from that dreadful saddle.

5

Dreamwold Was for Horses

At the same time Father was involved in the publication of his book, *Frenzied Finance,* he was at work on another project—his great estate, Dreamwold. He began developing the latter in 1901, at a time when we were spending our summers in Cohasset. We had formerly vacationed in Duxbury, also on Cape Cod; however, with Father's growing importance in the public eye it had seemed wise for the family to move to larger quarters for the summer vacations. We were so fond of the South Shore, especially the area around Duxbury, Cohasset, and Scituate, that Cohasset was the answer.

Father had purchased our Boston house from a friend, Dr. John Bryant, and one night at dinner he was discussing the move with Dr. Bryant. He said that he wished he had a house on the order of the Boston house but on the South Shore, where a large family could spend the summers. As it turned out, Dr. Bryant had such a house in Cohasset, only a few miles from Scituate and Duxbury.

I have never known my mother so pleased as on the day when we first saw the Bryant "castle." A winding driveway through a woodsy setting paralleled Cohasset Harbor, ending in a stone-walled courtyard. The Bryant house was most picturesque. Set on a promontory, it jutted into the ocean and was built along the lines of a castle on the Rhine. We all immediately fell in love with it. The ocean air had a marvelous effect on my mother's health, and for three years we rented this fairy-tale house. At the end of the three years, Father said,

"I would like to buy this house." We were all overjoyed, but a legality prevented the sale—the house could not be sold as long as Mrs. Bryant lived. Very sadly Father decided to go on renting, and he and Mother began driving around the South Shore looking for a site for a summer home. The following summer, they found the spot they were looking for.

Driving through the soft haze of a late summer afternoon, they came to a huge roll of landscape whose border was marked by a winding country road. Part rugged pasture land, part sheer rocky waste, and part scrub woods, the tract rolled over the country to a view of the ocean

The "Sunday flag" is flying over Dreamwold's landscaped lawns. This pole was one of the tallest Douglas firs shipped from Oregon.

Front portico of Dreamwold Hall, showing famous circular bed of heliotrope.

below the eastern slope. . . . While later developing this rugged piece of land which eventually became Dreamwold's thousand acres, Father's fertile brain had conjured up a much more comprehensive idea than just a summer home. It was to be a magnificent estate such as he had come to dream about.

Dreamwold Hall, built in colonial style, consisted of a main building and two wings joined at either side by passages. From the large entrance hall, doors at each end led into the dining room and living room. Connected with the dining room was a butler's pantry, a long room lined with cupboards that housed a priceless collection of china and crystal. This pantry, a long passage, terminated in the kitchen and servants' quarters. The living room connected with a narrow conservatory, library, and billiard room. Above were bachelors' quarters and guest rooms.

In the three main downstairs rooms, the woodwork had been chemically treated to tones desired by Father. The main entrance hall was very dark, almost black. The furniture matched the panels. The dining room was russet. This russet color was enhanced by Tiffany's creation, a lamp in the shape of a huge pumpkin, directly over the dining room table. The sidelights were also in Tiffany glass, depicting pumpkin blossoms. These lights gave a soft orange glow. At the farther end of the dining room was a bay window containing six or seven panes, with a breakfast table in front. The only ornament in the center window of the breakfast area was a famous bronze—Remington's Riders.

Pale fawn was the prevailing color in the living room and the furniture was oak. The most interesting features of this room were the pipe organ and father's famous collection of elephants, from all parts of the world, carved in ivory and of gold and silver. The andirons were designed by Father. Two bears in bronze stood on either side of the fireplace, depicting the ironies of the stock market—one bear getting all the bee stings, while the other bear was getting all the honey.

It was not until 1903 that Dreamwold was completed and the family moved in. It took some time for all of us to become oriented to the magnificence of Dreamwold Estate. As I have said, to Father it was the completion of a dream—the creation of a year-round home which he called his farm, but Mother never ceased to regret the Bryant "Castle of the Rhine." Perhaps this was because the castle was close to the ocean and high above the water so that it received a continuous crisp breeze; in any case, Mother's health improved while we were there. She was never as well at Dreamwold as she had been at Cohasset.

To Father, his successes were nothing compared to giving pleasure and health to my mother. However, it was ironic that with all his Aladdin's ability to grant Mother's slightest wish, he could not rub his magic lamp and give her back her health. He had begun to collect pearls for

Ready for a Sunday drive. Leaving front portico are Father, Mother, and little Bunny—along with properly attired coachman and footman.

"Dreamwold at Cape Cod . . . a place where Father could rest, enjoy his family, and raise horses."

her, choosing each matched gem from perhaps a hundred. When this rope of pearls was complete, it went twice around her neck. He then gave each of his daughters a necklace of perfect pearls culled from these collections of gems.

Dreamwold has been called a glorified farm, begun as an all-round country home. It was to be a place where Father could rest, enjoy his family, and raise horses. That he realized his dream of raising horses of a typical American breed was best expressed by his successes at the large horse shows. As Father once told a group of visiting German agriculturists,

"The aim of Dreamwold is to produce a perfect *typical* American horse for harness racing, show ring, family or pleasure driving, and the saddle horse—distinctive from those bred and raced in other countries, such as the English hackney, the French coach horse, or the Russian or Orloff trotter and carriage horse." Eventually Dreamwold housed three hundred horses.

One famous horse was Boralma, known as the Great Charity Horse. He was Father's magnificent three-year-old trotter, winner of the Kentucky Futurity in September of 1900. The $50,000 purse, my father gave to charity—$25,000 for a white children's home and $25,000 for a black children's home. When Boralma (fouled in his last race which the valiant horse finished with a cut tendon) was turned out to pasture at Dreamwold for life, many sightseers came to pay their respects.

This "retirement farm," looking like an English estate, soon became one of the showplaces of the country. Dreamwold Hall, built on a gentle hill, had a fine view of pleasant acres, dotted with buildings with gray shingles and outlines typical of Cape Cod; beyond stretched the Atlantic. It was difficult to realize how, in the short time of two years, a barren waste of stony, uncultivated land had been changed into a thousand acres of woodland, fields, rolling meadows and upland as pleasing to the eye and as soft as the rich landscape surrounding an estate centuries old.

An imposing water tower, often called "the most beautiful in the country," was one of the monuments of the engineering work on the estate. It was erected around an unsightly steel water tower and was a copy of an old fifteenth-century Roman tower. It stood 153 feet high. Near the top was a bellroom with ten bells, which automatically played the Angelus at 7 a.m. and 6 p.m. Directly above the bellroom was a giant clock which struck the hour. Completed, the tower is said to have cost over sixty thousand dollars. Later it was presented to the town of Scituate.

A visitor to Dreamwold would take the South Shore train to the little station of Egypt, twenty miles from Plymouth. Here he would go through the main gate, and following a broad avenue, would pass by the many

Water Tower at Dreamwold

"An imposing water tower . . . was one of the monuments of the engineering work on the estate. . . . Near the top was a bellroom with ten bells which automatically played the Angelus at 7 a.m. and 6 p.m."

stables. Flanking the avenue on the right was the "show stable." This building housed the blue-ribbon winners at one end—show horses, both for riding and driving. The coach house was at the other end and was completely filled with every type of carriage of the day—from the great glittering coach-in-four to the smart, dandy little pony carts.

Continuing on, the traveler would stop beside the riding academy. Here horses were trained for the show ring and the hunt. The tanbark ring was said to have been second only to Madison Square in size and construction.

Between the riding academy and the nine-hundred-foot racing stable stood the stallion stable housing stud horses of many breeds—racing, trotting and show horses; also the heavy percheron work horses. This stable was built in the form of an arc with small, high windows. The unusual structure was built to prevent the stallions from seeing each other, for if they did, the fight was on!

Beyond the racing stable, the winding driveway divided. One road wound on up to the right by the kennels, and farther on were the dairy barns and silos. Father's imported Jerseys were well known throughout New England—the dairy herd being headed by "Flying Fox," his fifty-thousand-dollar Jersey bull.

The Dreamwold kennels specialized in only two breeds of dogs, the English Bulldog and the King Charles Spaniel. My impression is that these spaniels are no longer

Looking down on Dreamwold Hall and landscaped lawns. There were flowers everywhere.

Driveway from Dreamwold's main gate past long (900-foot) stable for racing horses.

Beyond the kennels, the silos, and cowbarns was Dreamwold's second gate, on busy Plymouth Highway. Note the great water tower and flag, far left.

bred in England. However, since the beginning of the English Bulldog, the world had been compelled to go to Britain for its prize winners. It was Father's intention to invade the home of the English Bulldog with the American breed. Hopefully, the American breed could hold its own.

As in everything he did, there were no halfway measures taken to make his bulldog venture a success. He acquired champion English Bulls and went into the business of showing and breeding them. Eventually his bulls became renowned champions in the show-dog world. The Dreamwold bloodline is still famous and thriving in the breeding of English Bulldogs.

But dogs to my father were more than show pieces. He loved them. "The farther a man gets from the cradle," he wrote, "the less he thinks of his fellows; the nearer he gets to the grave, the more he hates his mirror and the more he loves his dog."[1]

His love for the English "Bulls" was never more movingly expressed than when he wrote:

[1] Lawson, *Record of English Bulls,* Egypt, Massachusetts, 1913.

"A Bull,
an English Bull,
for Mine!"

"The more a man chums with his fellows, the more uncontrollable becomes his desire to pal with his dog. Of course, I am talking of thoroughbreds, not curs. Although most thoroughbred, square-deal dogs have the count on men, there are dogs and dogs. For my part—and I have bred and palled 'em all—I say, 'The bull, the English Bull, for mine!' Take him all in all, he is the 'gent' of Dogdom. By that I mean that an English Bull, more than any other dog, will make a two-eyed, ten-toed man tumble deeper into his own littleness.

"Picking a bulldog is the same as picking a wife. It's a case of eyes—just eyes. If it's a pal for a dance, a wood-stroll, or a romp to the hounds, then tongue, form, and front may be taken into the reckoning; but when it comes to palling with a girl through the days and nights of a lifetime, then the picking must be done through the eyes, through that door to the long corridor that ends at the soul shrine—oh, well, I'm not so sure that dogs, English Bulls, haven't souls. I have one with a pair of great brown-brown eyes that open into a soul, or if it isn't a soul it is something mighty like what a soul ought to be.

"Of a night as he lies at my feet with his straight-gazing, never-blinking eyes between his paws, listening to the twelve strokes of midnight, he draws my look to his, and I see something in those brown-brown eyes that once, a thousand—perhaps a million—years ago, was in a form that sported cloth of gold and fragrant laces. And then—then as he sees what I see—he rises and lays his throat along my knee-cap and looks his 'Thank you, old pal, thank you' gratitude."

The Copper King at the entrance to Dreamwold Hall, with "Smike," one of his beloved English Bulls.

"Take him all in all, he is the 'gent' of Dogdom."

Returning to the left fork of the winding driveway, the traveler again leaves the stables and goes on to the half-mile race course with the judges' stands. Here my father with his friends would watch the running and trotting horses being put through their paces. Down by the racetrack, there was a deer park and you could see the deer as you went past on the South Shore train.

The farm included a nine-hundred-foot stable for race horses, a dove cote, houses for the employes and the farm superintendent, a sewage plant, firehouse, a tremendous riding hall, and a new post-office building for Egypt. The farm also had its house of economics—a pretty gable-roofed, two-story building that was Father's savings bank, which he had built for the accommodation and the encouragement of thrift among his employes. A Dutch windmill with its wide wings was one of the picturesque features.

The driveway comes to an end in front of Dreamwold Hall. Standing on the steps of the front portico, the traveler faces a broad expanse of emerald-green lawn bounded by a high hedge secluding the grounds from the busy highway to Plymouth.

On the lawn in front of Dreamwold, Father wanted to erect the tallest flagpole he could find. After much searching, the forests of Oregon were selected to supply the pole. As a result, a huge pole came across country on three flat cars—the largest individual stick of Oregon fir that had ever been shipped up until then. During

Father and Bunny in front of The Nest at Dreamwold.

The Nest was a replica of an old-fashioned Cape Cod cottage, covered with pink, rambling Dorothy Perkins roses. . . . "Father . . . loved flowers in a lavish way."

World War I, this staff flew the largest American flag in the nation.

At the time of World War I, a townsman said to my father, "Don't you think you should haul down that big flag of yours, Mr. Lawson? The German U boats are getting closer to the Atlantic coast. It would sure make easy shelling." My father's answer was, "I've never hauled down my flag yet!"

Father was a great lover of beauty in all things. Both Father and Mother were particularly fond of flowers, and our rose garden in Winchester was exquisite. One of my first memories was of trotting along with my father on a Sunday morning when I was about four, carrying a small basket. He would pick rosebuds, choosing them carefully, and I would place them in my basket. When we had a bouquet of perfect buds, I would take them up to my mother.

But, Father, besides loving these simple flowers, loved flowers in a lavish way. From the time we moved into the Boston house, Edward McMulkin, the head man for the florist, Thomas Galvin, furnished plants throughout the winter for our house. McMulken came every week with Galvin's flower van. He removed all plants from the house and replaced them with fresh ones. Those removed were taken back to the hothouse to recuperate.

We were still living in the Boston house when a new carnation was developed. It was large and its color

Bunny on the gate leading to Dreamwold's ten-acre garden, which contained a specimen of every shrub grown in New England. To Bunny's left is one of Tom Lawson's large collection of elephants, gathered from all parts of the world. In the left background is The Nest, where he did much of his writing; this was a replica of a Cape Cod cottage. In the middle background is the fire station, housing complete fire-fighting equipment and entirely man-powered. To the right is the Dutch windmill . . . Dreamwold, 1905.

bordered on a salmon pink. Mr. Galvin had spoken to Father about the beauty of the new carnation which was yet unnamed. Immediately Father was interested and when he saw the carnation, he told Galvin, "I want to buy that carnation and name it for my wife. I am willing to pay, whatever the price, to own the rights." Father paid thirty-thousand dollars for this fabulous creation—the Lawson Pink. From that time on, Father's many blue-ribbon horses never came into the ring without a Lawson Pink in their bridles.

Another of his hobbies was collecting unset gems. A jewel broker in New York would often call him about a new import—usually an almost priceless stone. In the dining room at the Beacon Street house, Father would sometimes have "the jewel trunk"—a small, old-fashioned steamer trunk—brought to the table and he would show us his latest find. I can see him now. Each jewel was wrapped in a little white tissue paper, such as old-fashioned powders were put up in. Carefully turning back the layers of paper with his short, stubby fingers, he would reveal a priceless diamond, sometimes a ruby, emerald, or sapphire.

Later, when his daughters married, Father gave us the pick of these valuable gems. "You are extravagant," he would remark, "which is my fault—but in times of stress when money is scarce, a diamond might come in handy." Aside from sentiment, he well knew that diamonds would increase in value with time.

Father admiring Gladys on "Gorgeous."

"My father's first pair of show horses were aptly called Gorgeous and Glorious. From then on all his blue-ribbon winners bore either Gorgeous or Glorious as a prefix to their names."

Winter 1904. Dreamwold's front entrance, showing in first sleigh, Michael Kelly on box, Billy O'Brien the footman, and Tom Lawson. Arnold is in second sleigh with groom . . . all are in typical winter garb.

In the 1920s, when money had become scarce on the western ranch where I was later to live, I sent back to Tiffany's in New York my unique and beautiful diamond necklace. Tiffany always gave a guarantee of buying back any valuable purchase, paying the current value. On this occasion they replied, "Tom Lawson bought this necklace in 1901; he paid then $2,300 for it. We now offer you $3,500." As Thomas W. Lawson had said, diamonds were a good investment.

Father was often called a financial wizard, but to his children, he was a magician. Wizard or magician, the most lasting of his creations were the weddings of his three older daughters. Take Gladys, for instance, who was five years older than I. She was the most beautiful blue-eyed blonde, "one of the most beautiful women of the day," according to news articles. It was for her wedding—October 11, 1905, my seventeenth birthday—that Father had spent months creating the first of his seasonal weddings for his daughters. There was an autumn wedding for Gladys, a summer wedding for Marion, and a winter wedding for me . . . but more of that later.

6

Boats Are for Racing

Father was a great believer in luck and seemed to bear an almost charmed life. He was also somewhat of a fatalist. The toss of a coin determined for him more than one stock transaction. He believed that whatever befell after a man had done his best was part of a grand scheme of the total of human events. He trusted in the good luck of certain numerals. The figure 3 or its multiple appeared in all his affairs. His office was 333 State Street; his telephones were 333 and 3339 respectively.

Always in high spirits and always on the move, he was subject to accidents, many of which involved horses or boats—both of which he loved. I remember one yachting incident that would have ended in disaster had it

The Copper King

Thomas Lawson in his State Street office, Boston, Massachusetts—checking stock market on ticker tape. Bronzes on desk foreground are famous leaders—Alexander Hamilton and Napoleon. J. P. Morgan's photo is on couch. Colorful flower bouquets were replaced regularly.

not been for his ability to make an instant decision and act immediately upon it. . . .

During the years when we were all at home, Father owned several beautiful yachts. Besides *My Gypsy*, which had been named for Mother, there was the famous *Dreamer*, which he commissioned and built when he moved to Dreamwold on Cape Cod. Earlier, however, he had rented his first steam yacht, the *Reva*, which he used not only for the family's enjoyment, but for entertaining business associates.

One spring evening, a group of Boston businessmen were meeting and dining with my father on the yacht. My brother Douglas and I had begged to be taken on the trip. We were enthusiastic sailors and Father's unfailing recruits on deep-sea fishing trips and simple pleasure sailings, but this time Father was adamant—"No children allowed!" We were lucky. . . .

Coming out of Boston Harbor and on toward the South Shore, the *Reva* ran into a dense fog. While the dinner was in progress, foghorns were wailing all around. Suddenly there was a terrific crash. The yacht shuddered. Dinner forgotten, host and terrified guests dashed up on deck. There, to their horror, they saw the Nantasket excursion steamer backing away from a gaping hole in the *Reva's* side.

In an instant, my father perceived the danger of the inrushing water and without a word turned and made

The Copper King's Cup challenger, *Independence,* on a trial run in the waters off Cape Cod. (The Peabody Museum of Salem)

"Of all Father's never-ending projects, one of the most challenging was the building of the racing boat, Independence, *to prove that Boston could construct as good a Cup defender as New York."*

a flying leap onto the deck of the Nantasket boat. From the *Reva* came a wild cry from the dinner guests,

"For God's sake, Tom, don't leave us to drown!" That was far from my father's idea, for striding up to the captain of the receding steamer, he shouted,

"Shove your bow back into that hole and hold it there!" While the frenzied crew on board the *Reva* worked with sandbags, blankets, and all available stuffing to stop the ocean from pouring into the *Reva's* great, open wound, the Nantasket captain kept the bow of his boat plugged tightly into her side.

There is a chilling aftermath to this story. In a picture of the *Reva* taken later, it was shown that two of its bedrooms had been completely demolished. Doug and I would have been sleeping in those rooms if Father had not been "adamant."

Of all Father's never-ending projects, one of the most challenging was the building of the racing boat, *Independence.* His fertile brain triggered the idea that Boston shipbuilders could build as fine a boat as New York shipbuilders.

In 1901, for the tenth running of America's Cup Races, Sir Thomas Lipton had brought his *Shamrock II* over from England to New York to again challenge American supremacy in this international event. Two American yachts were vying for the honor of defending the Cup—*Columbia*, two years old, the winner of the previous race, and *Constitution*, which was designed specifically to win the trials. Both had been built by New York's Herreshoffs. In the trials, *Columbia* was chosen to meet the *Shamrock II*. This is where the situation stood when Father entered the scene.

A syndicate headed by him decided to prove that Boston could construct as good a Cup defender as New York. All it took, he said, was wealth and will. He chose Bowdoin B. Crowinshield as designer and George Lawley and Brothers to be the builder. For several years he had been critical of the possessive stand of the New York Yacht Club group. Backed by Father, the Boston syndicate proposed to build a yacht to challenge *Columbia*.

At this point, although nothing in the rules said so, the New York Club stated that, to enter the race, Father and his group must surrender their boat to be raced under New York Yacht Club colors. Actually the only requirement was that the boats be within the waterline length agreed upon by both British and Americans.

Father was determined. He denounced the New York Yacht Club as an "enemy of democratic processes," and would not hand his boat over to them. He would sail *Independence* under the flag of the Hull-Massachusetts Club. He insisted that the Cup was an American trophy and should be free for any American who had the "will and the wealth" to defend. Furthermore, he proposed to fight for this end.

On June 3, 1901, the sails of *Independence* were hoisted for the first time off Boston Light. Sometime afterward, trials were arranged between *Columbia* and *Independence* by the Newport Yacht Racing Association, which was sympathetic to Father. Had the designer and crew of *Independence* been able to observe her in more than this one series of runs, several serious faults might have been corrected and the outcome of these trials might have been different.

Independence was "scow-built"; that is, her hull was shallower and flatter than most racing cutters at the time, and as a result, under proper conditions, she was faster, my father knew, than any other boat of her type. She performed best in a stiff breeze. Earlier, however, she had encountered heavy seas on a tow from Boston to Newport and her seams had opened. She was too lightly built and too heavily canvased, making her often difficult to handle. In her trials with *Columbia,* she won only one race and was eliminated.

When she failed in the trials, my sister, Gladys, was sure she had jinxed the yacht. She was eighteen when she christened *Independence.* Father had wanted everything as American as possible. The boat was named *Independence,* an American Copper King's daughter christened it, and American champagne was used. . . But the bottle didn't break when Gladys first swung it, and the boat did start sliding off the ways immediately after she pronounced, "I christen thee. . . ." So Gladys frantically grasped the bottle with both hands and swung again. Still it wouldn't break. By this time *Independence* was off the ways and the bottle had to be smashed with a hammer.

Later Father wrote the story of *Independence* and had a thousand copies privately printed. It was called *The History of America's Cup.* It is a beautiful volume throughout, magnificently illustrated on parchment-like paper and bound in heavy white cloth.

Father was afterward greatly criticized for his final treatment of his $250,000 Cup challenger. After the boat was dismantled, he had the hull of *Independence* broken up into firewood. Only her mast and sails survived the holocaust. To his critics, Father answered,

"I built *Independence* for a purpose. When she failed in that purpose, I had to have her completely demolished." But she was not completely destroyed. The beautiful white-cloth bindings of *The History of America's Cup* are cut from her sails and today one of her masts stands on a South Shore estate proudly flying the flag of the United States—red, white, and blue—Old Glory!

Father's active business interests resulted in the construction of yet another great boat. It was to be the only seven-masted schooner ever built. He did not own or commission this one, but his imagination was behind its construction, and it was named the *Thomas W. Lawson.*

It was built and launched at Fore River Works, Quincy, Massachusetts. The launching is still clear in my mind today, as Father and I had a slight argument over the event. I was twelve at the time and he had his heart set on his twelve-year-old daughter christening the seven-master. However, his daughter had a different idea. She burst into tears and flatly refused to crack that champagne bottle on the schooner's bow. Whether it was the loss of the champagne or a supposed indignity to the craft, I don't recall.

The *Thomas W. Lawson* was the world's greatest steel schooner. The unique career of this schooner interested all seafaring persons during the brief, exciting five-year period when she sailed the high seas; she could carry three times her own weight in cargo. She went down during her first and last deep-water voyage, in a ferocious storm off the shores of England. She sank on Friday, December 13, 1907.

And, speaking of sailing, it was during the summers we spent in Cohasset that Father decided to build the most modern ocean-going steam yacht conceivable. The *Dreamer* was designed by Lewis Nixon, of Elizabeth, New Jersey, who designed the battleship, *Oregon*. When completed, the *Dreamer* compared in size, equipment, and cost with the most famous yachts in American waters.

Dreamer was 182 feet in length with masts 70 feet high. She was designed for the greatest comfort not only

The *Thomas W. Lawson*

". . . the only seven-masted schooner ever built."

tern view of the *Thomas W. Lawson.* he world's greatest steam schooner, she uld carry three times her own weight cargo. (The Peabody Museum of Salem)

Interior of the *Thomas W. Lawson.* She went down off the shores of England in a terrific storm, December 13, 1907. (The Peabody Museum of Salem)

The *Dreamer*

". . . It was during the summers we spent in Cohasset that Father decided to build the most modern ocean-going steam yacht conceivable. The Dreamer *was designed by Lewis Nixon, of Elizabeth, New Jersey, who designed the battleship,* Oregon."

for the family and guests, but also for the crew. The owner's quarters consisted of two suites, one forward and the other aft. The forward suite had seven staterooms and two baths. My mother's was 17 x 12 feet. The after suite consisted of two staterooms and bath and a large library, 18 x 12 feet, with an open fireplace.

The dining salon was finished in natural wood and had eight observation windows, each 22 x 20 inches, with heavy French plate glass. Storm shutters fitted over these—each with a circular light eight inches wide—to be used during heavy weather at sea; for *Dreamer* was no fair-weather craft. She was built to cross the ocean in any weather. The salon was also fitted with an elaborately carved buffet and contained all necessities for a comfortable and elegant living apartment. Lighting at night was by a cluster of five 16-candle-power electric lights. The dining table was so arranged that it could be removed, and the room made into a lounge.

There was a beautiful and extensive library, reached by a passageway from the main deck. It was a cozy apartment, exceedingly attractive, with bookcases built into the walls. The wood used was golden oak. Across one end of the library was an open fireplace. French tile of an olive tone was used, over which was a specially carved mantel, the principal figure being a bear. On the mantel were three enormous tankards of ivory, most unusual in substance and workmanship. They cost $8,000; the body of the center one was a huge elephant's tusk, 30 inches high and 12 inches in circumference.

Even today some of the fittings of the *Dreamer* would be considered remarkable. There was an ice-making machine with a capacity of 300 pounds every 24 hours; under the forward hold there was a refrigerator, 20 x 12 x 8 feet, for the storage of fresh meat alone, and another large compartment for keeping fish. Forty feet was given up to purposes of provision storage. Many innovations were found on *Dreamer* which were not seen on other vessels except in the navy. She had an automatic recorder which registered the time and duration of every blast of her whistle. There was a tell-tale light on the bridge, which went out if either of the side lights went out, warning the man at the wheel. She also had an illuminated bridge dial and engine-room telegraph. Every part of the boat was connected with other parts by speaking tubes and annunciators. For instance, Father could talk to the bridge, the officers' quarters, engine room, and servants' quarters without getting out of bed. Wherever electricity was used for signalling or registering any of the ship's workings, duplicate automatic arrangements were provided.

The figurehead was a beautiful woman, *Dreamer*, in teak enameled a flesh color. The artist's model in clay cost $500. On deck were sailing models of *Columbia* and *Shamrock*, each five feet over-all. Her pennant was white with a blue center, on which stood a Polar bear—significant of Father's attitude "on the Street." In the financial world he was known as being opposed to raising prices—to "bulling" the market.

Though originally estimated to cost $160,000, *Dreamer* actually cost $240,000 when completed according to Father's fabulous plans. And it wasn't for racing either!

Outstanding in my *Dreamer* recollections are the Harvard-Yale boat races in June at New London, Connecticut. The traditional rivalry between the two colleges created an atmosphere of intense partisan excitement.

Preparations were under way weeks before we set sail from Cohasset for New London. It was a large and jolly crowd that finally assembled aboard the yacht the day before the races. Mother and Father looked forward to this event as much as did the young people. To Doug and me, still children, the celebration on the eve of the race was simply stupendous.

On one side of the harbor were the boats from New York, mostly representing Yale. Across the harbor were the boats from Boston, jammed with Harvard rooters. The entire scene was illuminated by rockets and shore-based fireworks. A cacophony of ships' horns, bells, and shouted taunts rose over the water accompanied by snatches of the song, "Fair Harvard," mingled with strains of Yale's "Boola Boola."

In the intermittent darkness, Colonel Ledyard's *Electra* (New York Yacht Club) stood out, her deck sharply outlined by blue lights for Yale. In contrast, the crimson lights of our boat, *Dreamer*, loudly asserted the supremacy of Harvard.

7

"Gypsy dying. Come home."

About this time, Father and Mother decided that the two older girls should have a trip to Europe. Wealthy young ladies of this era often made the "Grand Tour" to England and to the Continent. These trips were of indefinite length, depending on their purpose, whether social or educational—and on the pocket-book. For girls in the early 1900s it was not the prevailing custom to go to college. College-bound girls were known as "blue-stockings" and carefully avoided by the opposite sex. Dates for these girls were few and far between.

A Mrs. Maude Howe (John) Elliott, daughter of Julia Ward Howe (of the woman-suffrage movement), had, for several years, been taking wealthy young ladies on

European tours. Mrs. Elliott was well qualified to conduct these trips as she had lived abroad for many years. She was married to the American portrait painter, John Elliott, and they maintained their principal home in Rome. So Mother and Father got in touch with Mrs. Elliott and a trip was planned for my sisters, Gladys and Marion, after Christmas.

It was about mid-January when the little party, consisting of Mrs. Elliott, the two girls, and their maid, set sail from New York for Italy and the Elliotts' home in Rome. The two weeks' stay in Rome was a whirl of gaiety for the girls.

Maud Howe Elliott's continental excursions were a mixture of business as well as social ventures. She was a diplomatic matchmaker of some magnitude. Her young charges often returned to the United States engaged to titled Europeans. Rumor had it that if her matchmaking activities were successful, a handsome bonus would be in the offing! Having entree to all of the courts and embassies of Europe, she was in a position to introduce her young charges to some of the celebrities of Europe.

Leaving Italy regretfully, the Elliotts, Marion, and Gladys traveled north through Switzerland to Paris. Paris was a repetition of the Rome experience, only on a larger scale. The trip culminated in London, where the Elliotts had negotiated for a house on Hyde Park. For the following three months, life in London at the Hyde Park house, with its five servants, was like a storybook. At this time, wealthy young ladies traveling in England were often presented at Court, but to Mrs. Elliott's regret, it was out of season for Court presentation. My sisters' trip continued to be a round of excitement, and proposals of marriage were not infrequent. However, despite all the fanfare, both came back to America unattached.

My own first trip to Europe was unexpectedly short. Plans had been made for Marion and me to have a trip similar to the original one Marion and Gladys had with Mrs. Elliott. Since Mrs. Elliott was unable to meet us in the United States, Miss Agnes Oliver, a close friend and former teacher at Gilman's School, was asked to chaperon us as far as England. A friend of Mrs. Elliott's would then take us on to Rome. Although doctors knew that my mother's heart condition was growing progressively worse, they thought it unnecessary to alarm us.

The sister ships, *Saxonia* and *Ivernia* of the Cunard Lines, made frequent summer sailings between Boston and England. In 1906, the *Saxonia* would sail shortly after Harvard's Class Day. This particular sailing would be a gala occasion—more or less a large house party. With the colleges closing, professors, their wives and families, as well as students were looking forward to summer vacations abroad. Our plans culminated the evening of Class Day. In the twinkling lights of Harvard Yard, many dates were made for the *Saxonia* sailing, which was to be our ship.

The Copper King's daughter at eighteen. (London, 1907)

In preparation for the European trip, Marion and I moved in a world of excitement, which only increased as sailing time grew nearer. Once on board the ship, we were immediately enveloped in the friendly atmosphere of our fellow passengers. We were both about the same height. Marion was a brunette and I was a blonde. Our lovely clothes could have been used by a bride for her trousseau.

It was traditional, at that time, to wind up the many entertainments with a ship's concert on the final night aboard. Anyone with any type of talent, no matter how small, took part in this. A day or two before the event, Marion and I were designated to sell programs. By this time we had become virtual "pets" of the *Saxonia*. I remember topping my many sales with a five-dollar bill from an English Naval officer, who had been wounded in China and was being returned home.

In contrast to the gay evening of the concert, the next day's stop in Ireland brought us a shattering blow. A cable from Father was waiting for us,

"Gypsy dying. Come home."

After the ship docked in Liverpool, we took the first train to London, spending the night at Brown's Hotel. From there, we made reservations to sail back to the United States. The quickest boat was a German liner far inferior to the English ships. Coming back out of season, we found accommodations practically nil; the food was even worse.

Every evening, a knock on our stateroom door brought trembling apprehension, as the knock on the door meant to us a cable from Father. However, my mother survived this crisis, and when my brother, Arnold, met us in New York, his first words were, "Mother is alive, but you will be shocked when you see her. She has lost a great deal of weight."

I can see my mother today as we came into her room at Dreamwold. She was sitting on the side of her bed looking out toward the distant Atlantic Ocean. Her lovely curly hair was pulled back in a braid. Even in her weakened condition she broke into her familiar smile as her two wandering daughters came through the doorway.

My mother loved the smell of new-mown hay. While we were gone, Father had wagonloads of freshly cut hay brought over from Dreamwold's utility farm and pitched onto the large front lawn outside her windows. During the day, Father and my sister, Bunny, would pitch the hay back and forth and the fragrance would waft up through the open windows. In the remaining two weeks that Mother lived, not only family but also close friends, hearing of her serious illness, came often to Dreamwold. Sometimes they would join us on the front lawn with the haying.

I was seventeen when Mother died. Her illness stemmed from an early bout with rheumatic fever, leaving her with a crippled heart. Even though she had been

Father and Bunny.

"My mother loved the smell of new-mown hay. While we were gone, Father had wagonloads of freshly cut hay brought over from Dreamwold's utility farm and pitched onto the large front lawn outside her windows. . . ."

a semi-invalid for several years, we never visualized her dying. When her death came, in August 1906, Father was stunned. As for his children, we thought the world had come to an end.

The following October was to be my eighteenth birthday. This was the traditional time for a coming-out party and we had planned beforehand for a very gay winter. My friends were all having coming-out parties and Father and Mother had planned a very special party for me, but Mother's death left me very depressed. The doctor diagnosed me as being in a "state of shock." I shunned my friends and went to none of the social gatherings.

To keep my mind occupied, the family sent me back to school to take more courses. At first this seemed a solution, but it really didn't help. It was the family physician, Doctor Washburn, who noticed the too-slow improvement and suggested I be sent on a trip.

"Virginia Hot Springs might be the answer," prompted my sister, Marion. Doctor Washburn simply roared,

"No! We'll send that girl north! She needs to get away from this soft living and get out into rugged country where she can get the color back into her cheeks and perk up her appetite."

So, north they sent me. With Marion's friend, Mary Kellogg, and her mother as chaperon, we left by train for Montreal a few days later. It was mid-January and when we got off the train, even the first whiff of that cold, crisp air made me feel better.

We stayed a week in Montreal as Mary had many friends there. After the first night, we were invited by a young man Mary knew to join him and his friend for a coast down Mount Royal. The "coasts down Mount Royal" were famous. Two young men called for us in a sleigh. I'll never forget going up Mount Royal at night —the lights twinkling on the snow, boys and girls in their bright-colored coats, and many people wearing snow-shoes.

At the top there was a high platform, and gathered around it were the people who were going to coast. Most of the young men owned their own double-runners and there was heavy betting on certain well-known sleds. There were six alleys for six double-runners. You walked up to the platform, then stood there and awaited your turn. When our number came up, we four were standing together. . . . I didn't know these people very well; Mary did. Mary's young man flopped right down on his stomach on the double-runner and then Mary fell right down on top of him. Down went the other man and Mary called,

"Come on, Dorothy." I was completely horrified to see these people lying there like sardines.

"No, I am not going to coast with you." I was very stuffy about it—just the worst kind of a New England brat. They all called back,

"Oh, for heaven's sake. This is the only safe way you can go down. Don't you know in a few minutes the man standing up there will press that lever and all six double-runners abreast are going to drop together, shoot right out, and go a half mile across the snow fields?" Not wanting to cause any more of a scene and thinking, "You only die once," I dropped down on top of this unknown fellow.

All my fears and doubts disappeared as we shot out onto the frozen snowfields under the full moon. Those six double-runners racing side by side were quite a sight. The air was ever so dry, crisp, and invigorating. It was a wonderful experience.

When I was a child, a double-runner was always considered a very dangerous machine. It consisted of two sleds—one sled in front, a long, broad board in the middle, and another sled at the back. These sleds were connected underneath with steel runners which could be made to go very fast, as on Mount Royal. As long as one dropped into his particular alley, he was all right. However, if one double-runner happened to get out of line on the open snow and hit another double-runner, there could be a nasty accident. If one of those steel runners hit you, it could cut off a leg or even cut you in two.

After three days in Montreal, we went on to Quebec. There we stayed at the Chateau Frontenac, which overlooks the St. Lawrence River. The Chateau itself was

Dorothy and friend on silver tray, coasting at Montmorency Falls, Quebec, 1907.

Ice on the St. Lawrence River, Quebec.

"So, north they sent me. . . . After three days in Montreal, we went on to Quebec. There we stayed at the Chateau Frontenac, which overlooks the St. Lawrence River. . . ."

remarkable. The river was frozen then and guests could sit in warmth and luxury and watch, through picture windows, the activities on the frozen St. Lawrence.

The entire hotel was full of Canadians, for at that time of year, Parliament was meeting for the Province of Quebec. We seemed to be the only Americans there. Canadians we found to be most hospitable, and we made many friends, among them several eligible young men. Mrs. Kellogg commented one day,

"Well, Dorothy, you seem to be getting yourself engaged and disengaged at an alarming rate." Apparently Doctor Washburn's remedy had worked.

We finally left Quebec at the end of six weeks, stopping off a day or two in Montreal. However, before leaving Canada, we had made plans to come back the following winter. Little did I realize that before another winter rolled around, I would be starting out on another and longer trip.

8

Father Breaks the Bank at Monte Carlo

After Mother's death, Father was a changed man. His world was turned upside down. He seemed unable to recuperate. Then Gladys—the sister for whom Father had arranged the lovely harvest wedding—came forward with a temporary solution. Her husband would take a vacation from his business and they would try to persuade Father, along with my sister Bunny and her nurse, to take a trip to Europe. Father agreed; in his desperate mood he did not care where he went.

There were to be two parties traveling separately. Father's left first. With him went Gladys, her husband, Eban Stanwood; Father's private secretary, William Marriott Welsh; Bunny, who was nine, and Lizzie, her nurse since babyhood. Marion and I, with Aunt Mary and Swedish Jennie, the maid, followed shortly after. Mr. and Mrs. Elliott, who were in their apartment in Rome at the time, would meet our party there. We sailed from New York with a rather desolate feeling. For the first time in our lives, Father was not there to see us off.

It was quite a contrast when we arrived in Rome! There at the beautiful Hotel Excelsior, we had a great reunion with the rest of the family and a wonderful dinner that night; any affair he had a hand in must be lavish. This was to be his Roman Holiday. Even his mode of transportation was on a grand scale. At his disposal at all hours was a Victoria drawn by four black horses with black plumes—always used when Father set forth with members of his party for outings in the city.

Among Mrs. Elliott's many activities, besides matchmaking, was seeing that her young charge would be allowed to pursue her own interests. From her long life on the Continent, she was more than able to supply experts in every cultural field. This trip was to be different from Marion's trip with Gladys. Marion was oriented to the Elliotts' type of continental life; I was not. I was studious and my favorite subjects were languages and history.

Through Mrs. Elliott, I was introduced to an elderly English gentlewoman who was a well-known historian. This wonderful teacher re-peopled the Roman Forum for me. Three times a week, we would meet in the early morning and proceed to the Forum. During the entire morning, history would come alive for me and I would see not the visible ruins, but Rome in all its glory.

One of my most impressive Roman memories was having tea with Dowager Queen Marguerita of Italy, in the gardens of her lace shop. It was a lovely afternoon. Mrs. Elliott took us there and presented us to the Queen, who served tea and then took us through her shop. I still have a lovely lace collar I purchased there, also a parasol with inserts made of bits of her exquisite laces. They are still things of beauty.

One morning when we were in London, Mrs. Elliott warned us to take a little nap after a sightseeing trip because, she said, "We are going to have tea with a very interesting person." Even today, that little tea stands out in my memory as a brilliant highlight in my long life. Our guest that day was Mark Twain.

Some early mornings, Mr. Elliott would take me on interesting excursions while Marion was still sleeping. One such excursion took us to the gates of Buckingham Palace. Here Mr. Elliott stopped and gave me a short briefing. "We are going in here, Dorothy, to see a particular friend of mine who has some very fine Holman Hunt portraits. You have seen some of these in the studio, and I remember your enthusiasm over them. This, I am sure, will be a pleasure for you."

So in we went and I found myself, Dorothy Lawson from Boston, being seated at breakfast with the Duke of

Argyll, husband of the Princess Louise, Queen Victoria's youngest daughter. He was a charming, elderly gentleman and treated me as if I myself had been a daughter of Queen Victoria.

As time went on, Father's trip became even more splendid. Before going back to America he decided to swing around to Monte Carlo. As usual with Father, it was no sooner said than done. Marion, the Elliotts, and I saw Father and the rest of his party off to Monte Carlo. As the train pulled out, Marion said, "Good luck, Pa, break the bank!" Father's answer came drifting back to us,

"Yes, Marion, I will do just that." And *do* that he did!

At that time, in 1907, when one had made thirty thousand dollars betting at Monte Carlo, officials would announce "the bank is closed." Everything then came to a standstill as goggle-eyed spectators watched thirty thousand dollars being counted out to an unknown lucky person. Suddenly Father became that "lucky person." The "lucky fever" seized the entire party. Even my aunt, a conservative New Englander who disapproved of betting, placed her own twenty-dollar gold piece on a random number. The gold piece came back manifold. From then on Auntie's gold piece followed Father's lucky pace. The rest of the party was equally lucky, seeming to reflect Father's occult perception.

Father traditionally never kept any of his winnings, large or small; he believed that money should be kept in circulation—never stashed away for only personal advancement. When he broke the bank that day abroad, every cent of his winnings remained in Monte Carlo. He gathered his party together and they all went on a tremendous shopping spree. The ladies were showered with all sorts of delicate, expensive jewelry, while the masculine counterparts for the gentlemen were of their own choosing. Yet, no matter how exaggerated Father's antics were, we, his family, were overjoyed to see him regaining his old high spirits. Back home, he displayed his old vigor; his business interests were resumed and at long last he returned to his normal way of life.

About this time, there had come into being, in Chicago, on opera company called the Manhattan, headed by the famous theatrical producer, Oscar Hammerstein. Mr. Hammerstein hoped to present his company in Boston for two weeks, if enough financial backing were available.

Arrangements were made, and the opera would open in Boston with Massenet's *Thais* and Mary Garden in the title role. There had been a great deal of advance publicity and much controversy over the Manhattan's two outstanding numbers, *Thais* and Richard Strauss's *Salome.* Word had gotten around that Mary Garden would not be allowed to present *Salome* in Boston. A petition was circulated and presented to prominent businessmen, my father among them. This was the situation when Father, Douglas, Marion, and I arrived at the theater on opening night for the production of *Thais*. It was a gala night for Boston.

As the curtain went down on the first act, Oscar Hammerstein himself appeared between the curtains of our box. Beckoning to Father, he whispered,

"Will you follow me, Mr. Lawson?"

It was well into the second act before Father rejoined us, whispering loudly to Douglas, "Great heavens. What an evening! I have never been in such a place in my life." Marion leaned forward and carefully whispered, "Will you please be quiet, Pa?" But she had no effect; he went on,

"When Hammerstein asked me to follow him, I never knew we were going backstage. We had to dodge stagehands shoving scenery around when Hammerstein suddenly said, 'Here's Mr. Lawson, Miss Garden.' There she sat in all that makeup and practically no clothes, but there was no turning back. We talked and she pleaded with me to sign the petition for *Salome*. I was speechless and with the second act coming up managed to get back to you."

We refused to listen or speak to Father there at the theater or on the drive home. Narrow, bigoted young people that we were, we thought we were protecting our mother's memory. Next morning, Father, coming down early, said to Auntie,

"No breakfast for me, Mary, and I think I'll walk down by the river on my way to the office and not down the avenue this morning." Auntie was surprised until later when she saw the newspapers. Then she realized why Father had had no appetite for breakfast; he had seen them. They all carried glaring headlines, but the *Boston American* topped them with two-inch letters, "TOM MEETS MARY!"

Salome was not presented in Boston that year.

9

The First Time I Saw Paris

My romance with Hal McCall had its beginnings several years earlier. . . . His family and mine had known each other for many years in Winchester, but wintertime saw very little of the McCalls as the family then lived in Washington, D.C. Hal's father, Samuel McCall, was serving there in the United States Congress and Hal was away at boarding school. Since our family always spent summers on Cape Cod, the result was that while growing up, our paths seldom crossed until one lovely spring day when I was fifteen and Hal was attending St. Mark's School in Southborough, Massachusetts.

To me, Hal was a memory of kindergarten days until that spring day when I drove up to Southborough to watch a St. Mark's-Groton baseball game. With Hal being captain of the team, we were all rooting for St. Mark's, and were greatly excited over his final game of the season. However, our enthusiasm was short-lived, for St. Mark's lost the game.

Afterward, we rooters swarmed over to console the captain of the losing team. As we caught up with him leaving the field, I realized that this disheveled character was the blue-eyed little boy who used to drop me off at kindergarten in his pony cart. Simultaneously recognizing me, he smiled. The gloom began to disappear. Hal suggested,

"Give me a chance to clean up, and we'll all have dinner together."

After this ballgame, Hal and I saw more and more of each other. His sister, Katherine, was one of my best friends. She was my age, and horse-minded also. We spent much time together and one day she suggested that I come up and visit them the next summer.

The McCalls liked the mountains and their summers were spent at their place, Prospect Farm, at the foot of Mt. Prospect, New Hampshire. The farm was a gathering spot for young people of all ages. It was from there, in mid-July, that a postcard came to me signed "K." It proved to be an invitation to spend two weeks at Prospect Farm. I still have that postcard, but the handwriting is not that of my friend, Katherine. The signature was "K," but the card was written by Hal McCall himself. That postcard started a life-long romance.

When my train from Boston arrived at Lancaster around eight o'clock, I was expecting to be met by an enthusiastic Katherine. But, lo and behold, there was Hal McCall with a horse and carriage. It was a warm summer evening and the moon was getting full. Prospect Farm, I learned later, was two or three miles from the station. However, Hal McCall took a roundabout way, many miles longer through Jefferson Meadows, and we didn't reach the farm until midnight!

Two or three nights later, after Katherine and I had gone up to bed, there was a tap on the door. Grabbing a bathrobe, Katherine opened the door. There stood Hal and his cousin, Arthur.

"It's a wonderful night out, girls. Don't you want to come out for a walk with us? We can slip out through the back door of the kitchen. No one will know the difference."

It seemed like a wonderful idea. The boys went on down to the kitchen to wait while we hastily donned some outdoor clothes and heavy shoes. We joined the boys in the kitchen and went out into the moonlight. There we split up, Arthur and Katherine going in one direction; Hal and I in the other.

This idea proved so successful we continued our nightly excursions for the better part of a week. The August evenings grew more and more alluring and the

Hal McCall

"Upon graduation from St. Mark's he went on to Harvard. He was a star baseball player; the greatest second baseman, they said, in all college history. He could field any ball ever pitched."

moon continued to grow full. Two or three days before I was to leave, we four adventurers were dumbfounded as we crept back to the kitchen door to find it securely locked. At first the boys thought it was funny, but we girls did not. We panicked, for we knew we simply had to get into that house before daylight. The boys finally found a kitchen window open and gave us a boost, and we all clambered in.

After that summer, Hal and I saw quite a bit of each other. Upon graduation from St. Mark's he went on to Harvard. He was a star baseball player; the greatest second baseman, they said, in all college history. He could field any ball ever pitched. His slogan all through life was, "Keep your eye on the ball." After his graduation from Harvard, he was persuaded to take a trip west to visit a friend from Portland, Oregon. This was fine with both families, for Father had suggested a three-months' trip to Europe for me, during which I was to take classes at the Sorbonne. Before Hal left for the West, however, we had decided to be married the following January.

Plans were made for sailing from New York in September. A lifelong friend of Marion's, Roma Nickerson, a Wellesley graduate from Winchester, was to go with me. Miss Caroline Pond, also from Winchester, was to be our chaperon. Miss Pond was our piano teacher. Her sister, Miss Katherine, decided to come along too. Their brother was Mr. Handel Pond, who manufactured

Dorothy Lawson

The Copper King's Daughter dressed for a Harvard-Yale football game at New Haven. . . . "Before Hal left for the West . . . we had decided to be married."

a piano called the Ivers and Pond, which rivaled the Steinway at that time.

We four ladies sailed from New York on a beautiful September day in 1909, on the Cunard liner, *Carmania.* Father had made all the arrangements with Captain Barr. During the voyage we sat at the captain's table, on his right, and were treated just like royalty. After landing at Liverpool, we went up to Chester, and on to London. We stayed a few days in London, then traveled on to Paris and immediately started apartment hunting. We soon found one in a delightful little hotel, located on the Avenue d'Jena, just off the Arc de Triomphe, at the entrance to the Bois de Boulogne. Oddly enough, it was called the Hotel Roosevelt though not a person in it spoke English. The entire hotel was painted pale green; even the piano in our sitting room was a beautiful Nile green with gold trimmings.

Before taking up our studies at the Sorbonne, we made a trip through the chateau country. We hired a car with a chauffeur and every morning, after breakfast, we would drive around the countryside. Back in Paris, Roma and I enrolled at the Sorbonne. She studied art, and I took courses in French conversation and French literature. I also studied Italian from a woman who spoke only French and Italian. I could speak just enough French for her to teach me Italian.

On my twenty-first birthday, October 11, Father sent me five hundred dollars with the following message—

"This birthday money, Dorothy, along with a poem I have written for you, has been sent to you to buy your own birthday present. Since I cannot be with you, I want you to pick out something expensive and lovely and I *do* mean expensive!"

For several days after that, Roma and I traipsed up and down the Rue de la Paix looking in "expensive windows." Jewelry was our first consideration, but New England thrift won out. I finally decided on a set of furs—sealskin stole and muff for exactly five hundred dollars.

More treasured now than the memory of that long-ago set of furs is the poem Father enclosed with the birthday money:

To Dote on Her Twenty-first Birthday

'Twas back in '88 they tell it,
    They as saw the stork alight,
That the autumn's glow had faded
    In a soft October night,
When the bird pecked at the lattice,
    Pecked, and dropped his bundle white.

On the brown leaves and the red ones,
    On the velvet blades of green,
We opened up the bundle,
    And lo! a baby queen;
The pertest, prettiest morsel,
    Man or God had ever seen.

Since that soft October evening,
    One and twenty years ago,
You have rippled through our lives
    As a sun ray o'er the snow,

Till we scarce can comprehend,
You've been ranged by Cupid's bow.

Scarce can comprehend it,
That you, too, are taking flight;
That the nest will soon be empty,
That a shade will dim the light
Which has glowed so brightly,
Since that soft October night.

One of our greatest pleasures in Paris was the ice-skating rink, the Palais de Glace. It was as warm as a person's own home, and all around the rink was what would be called a lounge. There were couches and easy chairs where people could sit smoking, talking, and watching the skaters on the ice—and Roma and I were frequently among those happy skaters.

The railing around the ice was padded so that anyone just learning to skate could clutch onto the padding for support. We called these people "barnacles." They didn't dare let go, for they would fall down on the ice. There was a saying in Paris at the time that at two o'clock in the afternoon all the world—*le monde*—would come in skating. After four o'clock a woman was supposed to have an escort or a man skating with her because after four, the demimonde—models or questionable ladies—would come in dressed in evening clothes.

Besides the rink, we loved the Paris Opera House and spent many evenings in this wonderful place. Time sped by though, and soon it was the first of December. Roma and I then decided we couldn't possibly be home by

Christmas for we were having too good a time. We pleaded with the Pond sisters to stay on another month, but they firmly refused.

When it seemed as if we would have to go home, Roma ran into a friend she had met at West Point, Chris (Mrs. John B. Christian, daughter of the commandant of West Point, Colonel Sibley). Chris had put her two little girls in school in Antwerp, Belgium, as her husband had been ordered out to Fort Russell in Wyoming. She was then living in Paris and said she would be happy to move in with us as chaperon.

I wrote to Father and offered him a deal. I was supposed to come home to get married, but I said if we could stay on in Europe for three months with Chris as chaperon, I wouldn't get married for another year. Father was delighted and wired back, "Stay." The decision was reported in the December 12, 1909 issue of the *Boston Post*:

Miss Lawson Defies Ancient Superstition

"Scorning the time-honored feminine superstition that a wedding postponed spoils many a budding romance, Miss Dorothy Lawson—the third of the famous Lawson heiresses—has electrified a host of friends by putting off her much-heralded wedding to Hal McCall until an indefinite future date.

"It is now said that Miss Lawson has delayed her marriage that she may have the fun of an entire winter's travel abroad. The original plan was that Miss Dorothy was to be married in January. She herself set the event for that time, although she did not set the particular date. . . .

> "The engagement was announced some months ago and shortly afterward Miss Dorothy took an ocean liner, presumably to go to Paris to pick out the many frocks and accessories for her trousseau. The understanding then was that the wedding should take place sometime in January, and all the friends of the couple were looking forward to that day.
>
> "The engagement is not broken, Miss Dorothy has no Earl or Duke whom she prefers to the young American. That much is vouched for by all those connected with the family. It is only a postponement they say. Meanwhile, there is the winter season at the various European capitals, travel, excitement, and admiration before Miss Dorothy becomes Mrs. Hal McCall."

Chris, our chaperon, had been living in Paris so long she knew her way around, especially about the Opera House. She would stand in line for hours to get tickets for the performances. We always sat high in the balcony, for there the voices would rise above the music. We ladies had to take along some sort of smelling salts because the garlic smell was overwhelming. All the long-haired artists sat up there exhaling their garlic breaths.

Another pleasure we had was the pastry shops. In Paris they were called *patisseries.* Their windows featured mouth-watering round cheeses the size of automobile wheels. We would stop on our way home from the opera to pick up several slices of Camembert cheese and some French beer. We would then go home and sit on the edge of our bed eating cheese, drinking beer, and discussing the opera. After a month or so of this sort of thing and skating in the warm atmosphere of the rink,

I commenced to get run down. My left foot had started to swell and I didn't know what was the matter with me.

Nevertheless, we now decided to take our skates and travel into Holland. We would skate back and forth on the canals between the Dutch towns; surely the foot would get better there. As it happened, it was a warm year and not a canal was frozen. We went to the Hague the first night and then up to Amsterdam. By this time the swelling in my foot had grown worse.

When we got back to Paris, I went immediately to see Dr. Austin, an American doctor, recommended by our own Boston doctor. I had written Father about the trouble. Doctor Austin looked at me sympathetically and said,

"My dear young lady, I am sorry to tell you what is the matter with you, but you have the gout! It comes from either too much eating or too much drinking!" Under Doctor Austin's care, the gout was healed in a few weeks.

Roma and I would sometimes get together with other American girls and go to the concerts. One evening, she and I and one of these girls went to the Salle Gaveau. There a young violinist was introduced, just a little bit of a man, but he played many beautiful pieces. At the end there was thunderous applause and people gradually began to leave.

As the audience thinned out, the violinist stepped forward and played an encore. It was unfamiliar at the time, but today "Humoresque" has become known to all the world; also the name of Mischa Elman. As long as people applauded, Mischa Elman repeated his "Humoresque"; his final rendition being played to just three American girls.

At this time in Paris, the rainy season was starting and the rivers were beginning to rise. Roma and I, going back and forth to the Sorbonne, became aware of this rise because we always crossed a particular bridge over the Seine. This bridge was upheld by four huge statues. As we hurried across the bridge one stormy morning, Roma suddenly stopped,

"Oh, Dote, look down at those statues! The water is coming up over their feet!"

"Heavens, Roma, if this keeps on, we'd better get out of Paris!"

The next day, the whole of Paris was in an uproar over the flooding of the river. From then on, each time we crossed the bridge, we would stop and check our stone figures. Bit by bit, the river crept higher and higher. First the knees of the statues disappeared, and gradually the water rose to above the waists. Finally, before the worst of the flood, the figures were completely submerged. Meanwhile, I had developed a very bad cough and Dr. Austin seemed a little worried about my health. His advice was,

"My dear young lady, get out of Paris as fast as you possibly can. Take the earliest train to Switzerland."

Within a few days, we were on our way. As the train crept slowly out of the city, through the windows in the dusk we could see shadowy chimneys rising out of great lakes. It was frightening to realize those were the tops of houses. As the train started to climb into the mountains, the steep pull would cause it to shudder and then slow up. Each time it slowed up we thought, "Oh dear, it will never make it. We will all die here!"

Finally the train reached the top and we were happily breathing the clear, pure air of Switzerland. In contrast to the stench and filth of flooded Paris, our Swiss hotel rooms in Lausanne were a bit of heaven. Later we learned that our train was the last to leave Paris until the flood in France subsided.

After a delightful outdoor week of skating in Montreux and Vevey, we reluctantly left Switzerland and went on to Italy. There followed a few days in Florence and then we were on to Rome. Our stay in Rome was brief as our sailing date from Naples was the latter part of March.

The trip back to New York was in vast contrast to our pleasant crossing on the *Carmania* in September. We returned on a mediocre German liner which barely survived the "death-dealing" storms of the Atlantic. We docked in New York in a blinding blizzard and were told that the great Cunard liner, *Mauretania*, had just limped into port, badly battered by "the worst winter gales in history."

10

A Snow Wedding

When we were finally home again in March 1910, the newspapers came out with banner stories: I had not broken my engagement, and there was to be a large wedding. Spring and summer passed quickly as plans materialized for the winter "snow" wedding the following December.

After our engagement was announced the summer before, Hal and I had mapped out our future plans. His many years in Washington, D.C., had amply fitted him for a position in the diplomatic service. This type of life appealed to us both. It seemed to me, though, that his Oregon trip might weaken his interest in life in Washington. In the long run, this proved to be true. As Hal explained to me when he came home from the West,

"Will you agree to go back with me after we're married, Dote? I have been promised a job in Portland, Oregon."

After some protest, I capitulated to Hal's persuasion. "We'll go to Portland, Hal, but this move will be on a trial basis only. Will we plan to be home again for Christmas? If so, then we can make definite plans for our future." Hal agreed.

Father wanted a snow wedding for me, and snow he must have. When the great day arrived, December 15, 1910, no snow fell in Plymouth twenty miles down the coast and no snow fell in Boston twenty miles in the other direction—but at Dreamwold, great, soft, fleecy snowflakes fell from early morning until late at night. By the time guests arrived for the afternoon ceremony, cars were beginning to stall. From the entrance gates of Dreamwold to the doors of Dreamwold Hall, pink lights in evergreen settings glimmered on the snow.

In contrast to the quiet of the falling snow and the echo of the sleigh bells, all was hustle and bustle within the house. Maids were rushing back and forth to complete last-minute preparations. That day was to be the culmination of all Father's plans for my wedding. For weeks, workers—carpenters, decorators, florists—had been busy in our glass-enclosed east veranda overlooking the sea. Heating pipes had been installed and the floor covered with matting. The large room was decorated in holly, pine, and laurel. Through the lovely greenery shone soft pink lights, while artificial white doves hovered here and there. It was a veritable fairyland. In a far corner, partially concealed, was the orchestra.

In the forenoon, photographers, simulating the late afternoon ceremony, were taking pictures. Father, Bunny, and I, hastily attired in our wedding clothes, came down the stairs into the hall, posing briefly at the foot of the stairs. Turning from the hall, we came to the entrance of the now-transformed veranda. Ropes of roses and greenery bordered the aisle to the chancel. There we stopped for a final picture before the altar.

When we were back again in our bedrooms, Bunny and I took stock of our wedding finery—first the wedding dress. In far-off Paris, my dear friend and teacher, Valerie Menard, had planned with me the wedding dress. Yards of soft, ivory-colored chiffon velvet had been the base of Valerie's sketch. Now, in its complete form, it lay inert on the bed, all but its four-foot train embroidered in ivory-white and silver-threaded fleur-de-lis—the lilies of France. The Dutch neck and long, slender sleeves were banded in ivory-white baby ermine. Truly a dress for a princess!

The slippers were of ivory velvet, cut from the same bolt of velvet. Each slender slipper was embroidered with a lily, as were the silken stockings. Fastened to the Juliet cap of pearls was a white net veil edged with Point Venice lace. A string of pearls and an ivory prayer-book completed the bridal costume.

Hal McCall and Dorothy Lawson were married in Dreamwold's east veranda, overlooking the sea.

"The large room was decorated in holly, pine, and laurel."

Wedding Rehearsal

Father, Bunny, and the bride pose for photographers before the altar.

At four o'clock the strains of Lohengrin's wedding march announced that the "snow wedding" was taking place. After six friends of Hal's, the ushers—my brother Douglas among them—had seated the guests, the bridal procession came slowly down the rose-bordered aisle to the altar. There waited Hal McCall with his best man. At the altar, the Reverend John W. Suter, of the Church of the Epiphany in Winchester, was waiting to conduct the service. Bunny, in a white chiffon dress embroidered with pearls and holly, was my only attendant.

The music ceased and in a space of minutes Thomas W. Lawson had given his third daughter away. The Lord's Prayer and a benediction were repeated and then to the accompaniment of Mendelssohn's wedding recessional, the guests passed into the living room where a reception was held. Outside, the chimes of Dreamwold pealed forth the glad tidings.

Following the old English custom, the wedding day was a holiday for the entire Dreamwold estate. Employes had worked laboriously removing all the vehicles from the carriage room of the show stable. The floors of this great room, known as the coachhouse, had been waxed for dancing and a stage set at one end for the entertainment of the employes, their families, and friends.

When the bridal party with their friends arrived from Dreamwold Hall, the entertainment was coming to a close. Standing by the enormous Christmas tree set up

Copper King with daughter, Dorothy, at the "snow wedding," December 15, 1910.

"At four o'clock the strains of Lohengrin's wedding march announced that the 'snow wedding' was taking place. . . . The music ceased and in a space of minutes Thomas W. Lawson had given his third daughter away."

just inside the entrance, the party waited for the entertainment to end. When the curtain fell on the stage, the children dashed toward the Christmas tree and formed a circle around it.

Santa Claus was there in the form of the new bride, standing beside her husband. As each child passed by her, she handed out a Christmas stocking cram-full of gifts. During the remainder of the evening, the happy cries of the children echoed through the place, interrupted only by the strains of the music.

As the guests started to assemble, Hal and I took our places at the head of the line for the grand march. Once around the hall and the solemn music changed into the delightful lilt of a Strauss waltz. The merriment continued without a lull until half-past nine when a limousine drove up in front of the coachhouse. The young couple were leaving. Amid a shower of lights, the machine rushed into the night and was swallowed up in the darkness.

The "machine" which "rushed into the night" drove us back to Dreamwold Hall where Hal and I changed into our traveling clothes, mine of green velvet. The bolt of green velvet had come from Liberties of London, as well as the embroidered cloak. The plumed hat was from Paris, but the dress, cut from the green velvet, was made in Boston.

When Hal and I appeared in the hall, Father and Congressman McCall, who by this time were mellowed by wedding champagne, were waiting to give us their final blessing.

"Come on over here, Dote," called my father-in-law. As he took my hand in his, he said seriously, "You've had lots of beaux in your life, my dear, but you'll never find another fellow like Hal." (And I can even say today, at eighty-three, I never did.)

Father wrote a typical and tender postscript to the snow wedding and the lovely dance that climaxed it:

DOROTHY'S WEDDING DANCE

When today is dead and Memory's thread
Is tangled and ragged and bare;
Maybe from this sheaf will be culled a leaf
That will waken the day back there,
That will softly stir like the sighing fir
Sweet memories of an old romance—
That will waken again the gladsome refrain
Of our Dorothy's wedding dance.

Floodlights were shining through the snow as we stood on top of the limousine to wave goodbye to everyone. All the farm folk gathered around the car calling, "God bless Miss Dorothy! God bless Miss Dorothy!" That sound will always echo in my memory.

No one knew where Hal and I were headed for our honeymoon—not even his best man, who put us on the train for Maine. In those days, the Waldorf-Astoria Hotel was a popular spot for honeymooners, but Hal and I were great lovers of the outdoors. We had made arrangements to have my aunt's house at Mt. Desert Island, off the coast of Maine, and it was to be complete with housekeeper.

The honeymoon was a continuation of the snow wedding, but in a more primitive setting, for Mt. Desert Island in midwinter is vastly different from Mt. Desert Island in midsummer. In midsummer, the entire island bursts forth with what the native islanders call the "Rusticators," mostly rich New Yorkers and equally rich people from other parts of the country. Summer mansions along the shores are opened and Bar Harbor, with its golf course and hotels, becomes a New England Riviera. Palatial yachts and small crafts dot the harbors.

It was a brief but exceptionally happy honeymoon, and a healthy one as we spent our days snowshoeing and fishing through the ice. Back at Dreamwold we found the decorations had been left up from the wedding and the holiday season was in full swing. Festivities spilled over into the New Year.

11

From Cape Cod to Crooked River

There was a twinge of sadness as the last of the gay holidays drew to a close, for with the advent of the new year, Hal and I would be on our way to the West.

As I had never been farther west than New York City, the prospect of crossing the continent was overwhelming, but we went ahead with preparations for the trip and soon were on our way.

When we came into Portland's Union Station, it was a gloomy and drizzly January morning. There had been a gay group on hand at the South Station in Boston to wish us well, and I could not help contrasting our arrival in this strange and unfamiliar western city. From the station we drove straight to the Portland Hotel, an impressive edifice from the outside but a bit dreary on the inside.

Next morning we started house-hunting for an apartment. At the tag-end of the day, we found exactly what we wanted. We scarcely believed it—a spacious apartment with six rooms. Although the apartment was more than ample for our needs, it was difficult for me to adjust to the confinement of apartment life. Always before, I had spent my time in large houses or the great outdoors. I gradually became restless and unhappy as the rain never stopped.

New England's blustery storms were completely different; they were followed by clear skies. In Portland, the rain came quietly down and down—the wind never blew, the sun never shone. As time dragged on, the clouds seemed blacker and the rain wetter.

As I look back on January and February in 1911, one sunny day stands out in my memory. On Washington's Birthday, Hal played golf. The next day a violent pain in his head took Hal McCall to a Portland hospital. It was a recurrence of a frontal sinus condition.

Before coming east for our wedding, Hal had had an operation in Portland and this surgery was supposed to have cleared up the condition permanently. However, between doctors east and west, it was never quite decided what went wrong. The eastern comment was, "Not properly done"; the western comment, "Healed too soon." Another operation was recommended, and that operation changed our lives. The doctor's mandate was, "No office work for three months."

In the following interim, letters and wires flew back and forth between Portland and Dreamwold. The result was that Father and Bunny arrived in Portland in the late spring, planning to look over the situation for a few weeks.

On learning that his first McCall grandchild was on the way, Father changed his mind and decided to stay on through the summer. Ensuing days and weeks were gay indeed. The Copper King's reputation had arrived ahead of him—hotels were for sale, even entire railroads. Portland, the City of Roses, was at its loveliest and eager to welcome him. As the Copper King with thirty millions, Father was in great demand socially and commercially, as well as being newsworthy. The apartment telephone rang incessantly, flowers constantly arrived, and newspaper reporters mingled in the general hubbub.

Since invitations were plentiful from all around the state, a car and chauffeur were hired. One intriguing invitation was for a Fourth of July weekend in Central Oregon; we Easterners looked forward, with great anticipation, to seeing the cattle country. As we drove through the Crooked River Valley toward Prineville, I only half listened to the conversation, so intent was I on absorbing the passing landscape.

Oregon ranch country in early summer is unbelievably beautiful—no skies so blue, no sun so bright. First-cutting alfalfa is just beginning to blossom—fence high and emerald green—with millions of butterflies fluttering over purple buds. Great, thriving ranches sprawl on both sides of the road all the way into town. As we passed one field, Father was amazed to see, wandering loose in the expanse of green, a number of sleek, white pigs, both large and small. In Winchester, a pig meant a shadowy mastodonic creature kept under a barn, grunting and wallowing in eternal twilight.

The outlying Oregon desert is just as lovely, for the sage has a deerskin finish and the junipers a fresh, new-grown look. The eye follows almost limitless alfalfa fields, towering rimrock, and great stretches of sage and juniper to faraway horizons crowned by the snow-peaked Cascades.

We stayed with Portland friends at their ranch near Prineville, and it was here that my father became acquainted with the real West. Our weekend extended to a ten-day visit, which laid the groundwork for Hal's and my future.

When his other children were married, Father gave them houses and land within Dreamwold's thousand acres. This he had also planned to do for his daughter, Dorothy. However, after the visit to Central Oregon and Crooked River Valley, a seed was sown in my Father's mind. That "seed" proved to be his most fabulous project, and the one which has been most meaningful.

Excavation starts for the western home of Hal and Dorothy McCall, on Crooked River in Central Oregon.

Completed home on the ranch, where the five little McCalls—Tom, Harry, Sam, Jean, and Bebs—grew up.

In August 1911, 640 acres along Crooked River, in Central Oregon, were purchased by Father as a wedding present to Hal and me. Immediate clearing of the land, cultivation, and an irrigation system followed.

Hal made hasty trips between Portland and Prineville to oversee the work. Although I was feeling fine, with the baby due in late fall, my doctor thought it unwise for me to make these hurried trips. In Boston, the anxious grandfather kept the wires humming almost daily.

The three-story mansion in the sagebrush rose like magic in the shadow of the surrounding rimrock. Designed by a Boston architect, Ellis F. Lawrence, fresh out of Massachusetts Institute of Technology, it was a miniature Dreamwold Hall when completed.

Before Father left the West, we had made plans with him to have the baby born at Dreamwold. Dr. George H. Washburn, of Massachusetts General Hospital, and our family doctor would deliver the baby. Although Marion and Gladys had been married for several years, neither of them had had a child, but my older brother, Arnold, had children. Still, Father was both worried and excited over a daughter's first baby. Hal made the trip with me.

On the 6th of December, Henry, Jr. (Little Harry) came into the world, and there was great rejoicing at Dreamwold.

Hal stayed with us there till after the first of the year and then returned to Oregon to speed up final construc-

Tom Lawson on Dreamwold's front lawn, where he did some of his writing—poetry as well as prose.

tion on our western home. His letters from Prineville were glowing—he had started his beef-cattle herd.

In late spring, with the new house fairly livable, Hal came to take us back. Before leaving Dreamwold, Father called Hal and me into the library to say,

"Now that you and Hal are going to settle in more or less the 'wilds' of Oregon, I am sending out to Prineville a shipment of household goods. You will be far away from public libraries and the forms of entertainment to which you have been used. To the best of my ability, I will fill the gap. I'm sending you a large collection of games, an entire set of Everyman's Library (a thousand books), and also many fine books from my own library. I am sending, too, a miniature billiard table, and for outdoors, a set of English bowling balls for 'bowling on the green.' Sometime, not too far away, with plenty of water, you will have emerald-green lawn in place of dust."

Father gave us one more surprise present. It was the baby's nurse—a registered nurse from Massachusetts General Hospital. He said with a smile, "I want Miss Haggart to go with you and stay until you come back home again. I have made all arrangements with her. You are my fine and clever daughter, but you know absolutely nothing about rattlesnakes or babies!" The beloved Miss "Ha" (Miss Haggart) stayed with us long after Father had passed on. She became one of the family and an integral part of ranch life in Central Oregon.

In due time and with a great deal of hard work, our house became more than just livable. It became a finished product.

That first summer on the ranch, Hal and I had learned that our carefree fun-loving days were left in Boston. We owned 640 acres of ranchland, but we also owned 640 acres of ranch problems. We both realized that only serious hard work would make a success of ranching. The most immediate problem was water. Hal solved this problem with scientific irrigation. Water pumped from Crooked River through a large pipe into a main, canal-sized ditch turned dry acres into producing green fields.

When Father made a return visit, this time bringing Bunny, Douglas, and friends, there were again happy times. Luckily, the entire top floor of the house was livable, with white-washed walls, windows, and an easy staircase. Cots were quickly purchased, and the "attic" became the ladies' dormitory. The men were bunked throughout the house, Hal with them, and I joined the girls in the dormitory. Father was given the "master" bedroom. In those days, the east end was occupied by maids.

The following days were gay but hectic. Father hired a car and chauffeur from Prineville for the duration of his visit. We all traveled with him in trips around the country. On some of these trips, passing an alfalfa field, Father would have the car stopped, get out, and look over the fence. Now and then he found what he was looking for—pigs in clover! Furthermore, they were clean as newborn babes. It was becoming evident that pigs were taking possession of him.

When he developed Dreamwold, his "glorified farm," Father meant to have the best of every breed of animal. However, he overlooked the pig. The reason was that, to him, a pig was a repulsive animal wallowing in eternal muck. The idea that he had been wrong plagued him and he always meant to correct the omission when the opportunity arrived.

After Father and his party had left for the East, life became normal again and Hal and I began planning for our second baby.

Westernwold on Crooked River—landscaped by the ever-generous Copper King for his daughter, Dorothy.

12

Pa and Pigs

The coming Christmas would be my first Christmas in our new home. Hal would not be able to leave the ranch both in December and the following March, when the second baby was due, so the Christmas trip home was canceled. However, we Easterners staged a Christmas truly worthy of Dreamwold itself. Friends and neighbors from miles around were invited for ice cream and cake and to light the tree. It was an open house never to be forgotten. Guests began arriving in the late afternoon in buckboards, buggies, and haywagons. Many rode horses.

Far from New England there was little time for nostalgia, but as the festivities closed and Hal and I started

Arrival in the City of Redmond, January 1913, of Dreamwold stock for the McCall ranch, "Westernwold." The stock has just been unloaded from the eastern train. The sign on the wagon second from right reads: Dreamwold, the Farm of Thomas W. Lawson, to McCall's Ranch, Crooked River, Crook County, Oregon. The sign far right reads: World's Champions—Jerseys, Holsteins, Berkshires, Chestershires, Tamworths, Poland Chinas, Plymouth Rocks, Rhode Island Reds, Scotch Collies, Chesapeake Bays, English Bulls, Royal Siamese Field Ratters.

up the stairs, we turned for one last look at the remains of our first Christmas in the West. Firelight still cast shadows on the ceilings and on the one little white sock hanging beneath the mantel of the living-room fireplace.

Before we started east in February 1913, for the birth of little Tommy McCall, Father shipped us a carload of valuable stock from Dreamwold. Work stopped on the ranch when word got around that the stock was arriving. All hands gathered around the cow barn as the loaded trucks rolled from Redmond. Every species of animal from Dreamwold was included in the shipment, and buildings were well prepared for the registered Jerseys, standard-bred trotting horses, South Down ewes and rams, and finally the cages with Rhode Island Red and Plymouth Rock hens and roosters.

That was in January; the following month Hal and I headed east for me to keep my date with the stork. Hal returned first; he didn't want to be gone long from the ranch and its new inhabitants—but it was more than two months before the mother and Oregon's future governor, nine-pound baby Tommy, were pronounced ready for the long trip west.

The Copper King had long wanted to spend more time at Westernwold, as we had named our ranch, and he finally made the decision the following year. At that time, April 1914, I was again at Dreamwold having our third child, little Dorothy. Hal had already gone back to the ranch as spring work was at its height. While

I was convalescing, Father and Auntie came to the decision to make the trip back to the ranch with the baby and me.

As usual, the trip was lavish; Father and his party took over the better part of an entire parlor car. He had one stateroom and Auntie and I, with the baby, had the other. The party also included Miller, Father's English secretary, and the baby's nurse, who went as far as Chicago with us. Our arrival at the Blackstone Hotel in Chicago was another Roman Holiday. We trouped into the lobby of this glamorous hotel like visiting royalty. Here, again, Father took over. We were already familiar with the Blackstone as it was our third trip east, returning each time with a new baby. After the last trip, we had come back with new-born Tom.

The baby's nurse accompanied us as far as Chicago; after that our only help was the English secretary, Miller, but by the time we reached the ranch, Miller had become a better baby sitter than the nurse. When we went into the dining car, Father would say,

"Miller, would you mind the baby?" And that dignified Englishman would lean over the crib and start tickling the baby's nose. The transformation was amazing.

Father planned to spend at least three or four months at the ranch; at the end of four weeks, my aunt went back without him. Father stayed with us on the ranch for one full year, from April 1914 to April 1915.

After Mother's death, he had become a very somber man. He had worn nothing but black and vowed he would never wear colors again. However, when he started for the ranch in 1914, he was equipped with a wardrobe fit for a movie actor. In his well-tailored, western outdoor clothes, he presented a striking figure. To the neighboring ranchers, his custom-made corduroys were merely a different version of their own outfits. He was a genial man and easy to know. He loved the outdoors and outdoor people.

After Auntie had left for Boston, Father began seriously working on the "pig project." Our ranch livestock then included everything but pigs—which became Father's opportunity to help us further with our livestock business. Hal, though, was dubious about pigs, and would argue with Father,

"But, Mr. Lawson, why not invest your money in cattle?"

"It takes a cow, Hal, nine months to have a calf; pigs farrow three times a year. I want action, Hal, action!"

The 160 acres adjoining our ranch to the east were on the market. Hal and Father looked into the possibilities of this investment. After due consideration, the decision was made to buy this additional acreage.

Father went into the project with his usual enthusiasm and energy. Money being no object, buildings rose like magic and a mass of workers were put on the land. Only registered hogs were to be raised on the ranch,

The ranch's Octagonal House, to accommodate pigs—and people!

"Only registered hogs were to be raised on the ranch, and they were to be provided for in the style to which they soon grew accustomed." (The large bell on the roof rang to summon hogs at mealtime.)

and they were to be provided for in the style to which they soon grew accustomed.

With his almost uncanny intuition, Father had selected just the right man for the development of his project, Lou Reed of Redmond, Oregon.

His daughter, Helen—now Mrs. Devere Helfrich—recalled for this book some details of the unusual building that was to house the Reed family and also accommodate the Copper King's hogs:

"I was seven years old when we moved to the ranch in the early summer of 1914. . . . I'll never forget my surprise at the shape and height of the house in which we were to live. It was new and we were the first to live in it. Octagonal in shape and two stories high, it sat on a concrete slab also octagonal, which extended twelve or fourteen feet out from the house on all sides. Around the edge of the slab was a groove or ditch in the concrete for drainage. The house was designed with bins in the bottom portion, the first floor, with living quarters above.

"The bins, seven in number and occupying seven of the flat walls of the octagonal building, were to hold the grain for Tom Lawson's hogs. On the outside of each of these seven flat walls there was a chute to be opened to let the grain spill onto the concrete, where the hogs were to be fed. This was then to be hosed off and the ditches around the edges were to carry the waste away.

"The eighth flat-walled section was left empty. It had a door to the outside and a spiral staircase which led to the living quarters on the second floor. A flat, asphalt-covered roof with a railing topped this strange building. Here there were lines for drying clothes, a sliding top on a stairway leading from the second floor to the roof, and a tall tower with a bell in it.

"I remember one time when Mr. Lawson was wearing a bright pink satin shirt and I was really awed by his fine appearance. He was inspecting the various hogs and when he came to one pen with a large boar in it, my father cautioned him about going into the pen. This particular boar was quite mean. Mr. Lawson, however, wanted a closer look and went into the pen. The boar went, 'Whoof, whoof!' and took a run at him, and over the fence went Mr. Lawson in a flash of pink satin. He was very agile, I thought."

Miller had been brought along to keep him in touch with his Boston office through correspondence and long-distance telephone calls. Meanwhile, the stock market veered up and down, mostly down, but telegrams and emissaries to the ranch made no impression on Father.

The condition of the stock market, from war rumors in Europe, had caused Father's office to panic. Eventually, my brother, Douglas, was dispatched to alert Father to the seriousness of the situation. Douglas's mission to the West was to bring Father back to Boston.

Thomas W. Lawson, the Copper King, at the peak of his career, 1913-1915.

"Banker, broker, yachtsman, author, and pamphleteer of Boston, Cohasset, Winchester, and Scituate."

However, when he appeared at the ranch, in the middle of Father's pig project, he was greeted with Father's ultimatum,

"I've made up my mind, Douglas. Stock market or no stock market, I'm going to stay and enjoy myself with my grandchildren."

Instead of being irritated by Father's answer, Douglas seemed fairly pleased and he himself decided to stay on a few days. Maybe Father would change his mind—but Father didn't. On the contrary, he just settled down to his newest enterprise—the raising of pure-bred hogs.

Scores of letters were being dictated by Father to Miller. These did not pertain to Father's stock-market business. Miller's daily letters were written to pig breeders and manufacturers of pig equipment throughout the United States.

In answer to the letters, pigs and pig equipment began to arrive. Unfortunately, the pigs arrived before the equipment. Father's error was in not knowing the difference between hog raising and that of other livestock. He realized that the pigs would arrive before the equipment or the buildings were completed, but in spite of this, he thought that with warm weather, the pigs could be placed temporarily in pasture like other stock.

Eventually, the hogs arrived. The best of every breed was represented. There were Chester Whites, Black Poland Chinas, and Brown Duroc-Jerseys; also Yorkshires and Tamworths (the English bacon pigs). And last, there were the Berkshires and the white-belted Hampshires.

There was great excitement with the arrival of the first sow, and from then on the excitement mounted. With the subsequent arrival of more sows and boars, the pig population exploded; but the inadequate housing brought about a grim situation. Temporarily most of the hogs were housed in individual, six-foot galvanized tin houses, with the overflow placed in surrounding pastures. One such overflow group was moved onto our green-lawn tennis court at the west end of the house. . . .

As we later learned, pigs are nocturnal. Unlike cows and horses, in the middle of the night they become super-active—squealing, grunting, and fighting. At midnight on the first night, I was jolted out of a sound sleep by some such hullabaloo.

"Hal, Hal, for heaven's sake, get up and see what's happening!"

Drowsily Hal answered, "Oh, go back to sleep, Dote. It's only the pigs on the tennis court."

Next morning, on my complaint, there was assurance that the pigs would be speedily removed.

On the second night, however, Father and I came to grips. Around midnight, the disturbance began. I jumped out of bed and pounded on Father's door. When he appeared in the doorway, he said,

"What in heaven's name is the matter, Dorothy?"

"I just want you to know, Pa, either the pigs leave the tennis court, or I leave the house!"

Pulling on his dressing gown, Father stalked by me. Picking up a baseball bat from the hall closet, he disappeared into the night.

Wondering about the baseball bat, I went back to bed. The sudden quiet on the tennis court kept me from sleeping. Soon I heard a scurrying sound and a squeal and a grunt. This was followed by a soft thud. Then all was silent. The same series of happenings was repeated over and over.

Toward morning my weary father left the battlefield. Later, at breakfast, he made a declaration,

"I want you to know, my girl, I'll never spend another night like that! The tennis court will be cleared this morning!" Father had spent most of the night "rapping" the hogs into slumberland.

As the pig drama unfolded, Doug gradually became interested in the project; so interested, in fact, that he started a project of his own. His "plant" was across the river in the willows. Here he kept several sows. Of course, Father thought that Doug's "plant" was just a passing fancy — as being midwife to pigs was quite a switch from the football field of Harvard College. Finally, though, he began to take his son seriously when he realized that Doug was spending most of his time with the sows, especially at farrowing time. Under Doug's tender care, the newborn piglets thrived. In good weather or bad, expectant sows were served their boiling water several times a day. Sometimes Doug did not come home until midnight; then he would leave at the crack of dawn, depending on what was going on in the maternity ward. He gave up shaving, grew a beard, and seemed to lose all interest in his personal appearance.

In the midst of all this, another emissary arrived from the East. It was my older brother Arnold, who had come in person to drag Father back to his business in Boston. When the telegram came, advising us of his arrival, Doug hurried over to Redmond to meet him. Arnold—who had spent much of his life in England—stepped out onto the Redmond station platform in clothes fresh from London: topcoat, derby hat, and cane. Doug clambered up the steps of the platform, still wearing his "maternity outfit" of battered sombrero and muddy boots. Grabbing Arnold by his immaculate English sleeve, Doug muttered,

"For God's sake, Arnold, swallow that cane or they'll lynch you out here!"

After the initial shock, Arnold stayed two weeks at the ranch. He was a great horseman and outdoor man—this side of the ranch appealed to him. But he disliked the isolation and the necessity of a daily routine. As an "emissary" he was a failure, for he went back to Boston alone. Father was currently more absorbed in the western stock than the eastern stock market.

The children's nursery at Westernwold. The large, stuffed animals were the Copper King's gift to his grandchildren, Tom, Harry, Bebs, Sam, and Jean.

Christmas of 1914 at the ranch was truly a festive family occasion. Stock markets were forgotten while Father enjoyed his grandchildren. That winter, Christmas off in the western sagebrush hills was almost a duplicate of our traditional New England Christmases.

Shortly after the holidays, Father, who was greatly impressed by Doug's interest in ranching, decided to buy him a place of his own. Doug was delighted and he and Hal started out looking at ranches. The news that millionaire money was loose in Central Oregon spread like wildfire. Potential sellers swarmed out to the ranch.

They finally decided on a promising ranch up above Prineville on Crooked River. Father insisted on equipping it with Percheron horses. This triggered another argument on stock raising.

"Why not cattle, Mr. Lawson?" Hal asked. "After all, this is cattle country, and Doug might as well make money on his investment."

Father disagreed. "It would seem to me, Hal, that heavy horses in this country would be a good investment. Doug certainly knows horses and should be able to make a go of it. So, Percherons it was and Doug started out with a thriving business on his new ranch.

By early February of 1915, the pig business was straightened out and even Doug's little "plant" across the river was successfully producing, much to Father's amazement.

On February 26, 1915, Father's birthday, we planned a surprise party. A group of intimate friends were invited, and the decorations for the dinner were lavish. Yellow chrysanthemums were brought in from Portland, and even though winter was still with us, the theme of spring yellow was predominant.

After a jolly gathering of the guests in the living room, all were invited into the dining room. In front of Father's place was a huge silver platter strewn with yellow chrysanthemums. In the midst lay a sleeping, creamy-white piglet. Around its neck was a large yellow satin bow, and on his diminutive tail a tiny yellow bow. The uproarious laughter of the guests scarcely disturbed the piglet's slumber.

Douglas, dressed for the occasion, but still with whiskers, was the master of ceremonies for the evening. His scraggly whiskers were tied through with narrow yellow ribbon bows. Before the applause subsided and the guests were seated, Father turned to my brother,

"Douglas," he said, "if you will go upstairs and shave off those whiskers, I will give you $1,000." I think even the baby pig awoke at that!

But my former Harvard and now hillbilly brother flatly refused the offer.

Before Douglas removed the little pig from the table and placed him in a blanket near the hearth, he turned to Father,

"I dub this pig Percy, and I want you all to address him as such." So Percy was christened on my Father's birthday and Percy he remained until the end of his days.

Percy would never associate with other pigs. He considered himself one of the family and took up residence on the lawn in the backyard. Naturally he grew to mammoth proportions, and finally, on one sad day at the ranch, it was decreed that Percy must go to market. We all felt we had lost a relative!

13

End of an Era

At the ranch, Father was constantly in the news. Guests from all parts of Oregon trouped in to visit him.

As long as daylight lasted, activities were mostly outdoors. Besides the grass tennis court, we now had a velvet-green lawn half an acre in size. The principal attraction for the men was "bowling on the green," and Father, with his flair for competitive games, would offer prizes.

For those not interested in bowling, there were horses of all types—fine Eastern saddle horses, Western stock, and ponies for the children. Not a day went by that there was not some type of horse tethered at the back fence.

Sunday afternoons were followed by buffet suppers in the kitchen. From Sunday afternoon until Monday, maids were given the day off and Douglas took over as chef. His main dish was a reheating of Saturday's baked beans. He used a huge frying pan and to this day no one knows the recipe for his gourmet seasonings.

After dark, some guests would settle in the dining room for bridge. The more lively ones took part in charades. During this game, some remarkable actors and actresses were discovered. Many who took part in those Sundays on the ranch are now gone, but I feel that among those who are left, there are still warm memories.

Father soon became a familiar figure, prowling around the ranch at all hours. Every morning after breakfast he would take one of his prized shotguns and start out for the river sloughs. Wild ducks were plentiful on Crooked River as well as other types of game birds. Sometimes he would be gone the entire morning and somehow he never came back empty handed. When the back door opened there would be Father with a string of ducks. He'd announce,

"Well, it certainly was good shooting this morning!" We could scarcely believe that, even with all his skill, he had suddenly become such a marksman. Then one rainy morning, Claude Butler, a neighbor boy, knocked on the door and asked,

"Where is Mr. Lawson this morning? Doesn't he want any more ducks?"

Embarrassed, but with a hearty laugh, Father said,

"Well, the truth is out and you've caught me red-handed. I've been trudging down to the river every morning in hopes of bringing down a few ducks. My only target so far is a humpback duck that lives in the corner of the slough. That duck seems to bear a charmed life. Claude discovered me one morning as I was drawing a bead on him. Before I could fire, though, Claude's string of ducks caught my eye and I made him a proposition.

" 'How about selling me those ducks, young man?' Claude was quick to accept the offer, and that's the story!"

We had many spirited arguments before Father left for the East. Hal and I were surprised one morning to see a shiny new Buick at the gate. We both thought more friends had arrived unexpectedly. We hurried out to take a closer look as Father called down from the upstairs window, "How do you like it, Dorothy?"

Suddenly on the door of that fancy little Buick, the large initials "DLM" caught my eye. The same thought struck both Hal and me—Father wanted a glamorous car for his glamorous daughter! But, surprisingly, his daughter thought differently.

"If we keep this car, Hal, we will be just too popular. The ranch will go down the drain while we are touring friends around the country." Father, still at the window, called down,

"What's the problem? Don't either of you want to get in and take a ride?" Hal hurriedly went on to explain,

"Would it be possible, Mr. Lawson, to trade this car in on a Buick truck? We need one more than anything else on the ranch."

"Slam" went the window. Shortly after, Father came down to the gate. He was not only hurt, he was indignant, but as Hal went on he began to understand our problem and finally agreed to the deal.

By the spring of 1915, Father began to receive urgent messages from the East—he "must return" to his office. Following a number of these messages, he sadly began making plans for his departure. The lack of material returns on his western investment he seemed to regard as incidental. It had been a wonderful year on the ranch with all of us, but especially with his grandchildren. By this time, Father had fallen in love with Oregon.

It was agreed that Douglas would make a hurried trip home with Father to settle his own affairs and then return to his ranch.

The house that Doug was building was nearing completion and Hal and I started making frequent trips to

Prineville in Central Oregon, July 1914.

". . . the old Prineville Hotel was the center of much activity, both political and social. The main street of Prineville was typically western, dusty, and drab, but the hotel's linoleum floors were spotless. The fun-loving eastern imports spent almost as much time dancing on those linoleum floors as they did working their irrigation ditches."

inspect the progress. Doug had many friends eager to help with the furnishings and decorations. It was then that the Buick truck really came into its own. Planks were placed across the back end, and with this makeshift arrangement and three in the cab, we could transport around fifteen persons. So Father really had the last laugh. If we had kept the shiny little Buick, we would never have had the problems of the overloaded truck!

When Doug came back from Boston, the gay days continued. During this period, the old Prineville Hotel was the center of much activity, both political and social. The main street of Prineville was typically western, dusty, and drab, but the hotel's linoleum floors were spotless. The fun-loving eastern imports spent almost as much time dancing on those linoleum floors as they did working their irrigation ditches.

When stockmen went down to Portland on cattle business, they usually stayed at the Imperial Hotel, but when excitement-seeking ranchers went down to the city on weekends, they would put up at the newly built Benson. Through hunting and fishing season, the tide turned; visitors from the "big city" poured into Central Oregon. Despite our increasing responsibilities, Hal and I would try to join the latter group on special occasions.

We were looking forward to a reunion with Father and the family during the Christmas holidays of 1916. We tried to talk Doug into going back with us, but he was too happy with his ranch. All arrangements had been made for the trip; our house was ready to close; furniture was covered with sheets, and the two maids had been promised an extended Christmas vacation.

The day in late November before we were to leave, a telegram came saying that Hal's father, Governor-elect Samuel W. McCall of Massachusetts, was en route to the ranch for a brief visit. This news completely disrupted our plans. The maids cancelled their holiday, the furniture was unfrocked, and the house began to bustle with preparations for Grandfather McCall.

The trip west followed immediately on the heels of Mr. McCall's successful campaign for the governorship. He arrived with his campaign manager, Charles Baxter, several days after we received the telegram, but could stay only a few days.

As so many of our neighbors were anxious to meet Hal's father, we held an open house on the Sunday before he left and asked a few close friends to stay for dinner. After some of our guests left, Mr. McCall sat back in a big armchair before the fire and looked at his son.

"Well, Hal, I can't tell you how impressed I am with the young men you had here this evening. Do you realize that way out in this pioneer country, every fellow here tonight was a college graduate?"

Our trip back east in 1916 was the last we made before the United States entered World War I in 1917.

Dorothy, during a visit to Dreamwold, posed for this portrait with the first three little McCalls: three-year-old Tommy (present Governor of Oregon), two-year-old Bebs (young Dorothy), and four-year-old Harry. The twins were not yet born.

"Our trip back east in 1916 was the last we made before the United States entered World War I in 1917. . . ."

The allies were suffering severe setbacks; the odds were against them. An intensive Red Cross Drive was under way in the United States for money to buy food for starving Europeans. The drive reached into every corner of the country, even the most isolated spots.

A Prineville friend, who was spending countless hours soliciting for the drive, told me of a heartwarming experience he had had when traveling the country above Prinevillle.

"There was one little old place I deliberately passed up. I knew about the family. The parents were hard-working, poor as paupers, with several kids. So I didn't want to embarrass them. But, believe it or not, coming back into town on that trip, I was flagged down by a woman at that farm gate. She was signalling me to stop. We exchanged greetings and she asked,

"You're travelin' for the Red Cross, ain't you? Well, here's our share." Then she handed me five one-dollar bills. "One of 'em's for me, one for the man, and one apiece for the kids."

The gay days came to an abrupt end when Douglas, being a member of the Massachusetts National Guard, was called up for the trouble with Mexico. At the end of this conflict, he volunteered to go into World War I, and was ordered back to Massachusetts for more training. With the rapid sequence of events, Douglas had no time to get back to his ranch. When Doug left for

Mexico, we had a rousing farewell party with his special friends the evening before he left.

With Douglas in Europe, Hal's responsibilities were doubled as no arrangements had been made for the disposition of Doug's ranch. Also, we were facing another trip to Dreamwold for the birth of a new baby. Finally, by early June of 1919, we were on our way east for the event. Since the baby was not supposed to arrive until the latter part of July, Hal returned to the ranch. However, the earlier birth the first part of that month created a crisis at both Dreamwold and the ranch. Summoned by an emergency telegram, a haggard Hal McCall was back at Dreamwold a few days later. To his amazement, he found two babies instead of one! Also, he was greeted by Doctor Washburn's decree, "Dorothy has had a rough time of it, Hal, and I think she should stay on here awhile."

Hal agreed and again returned to the ranch alone.

In the meantime, my sister Bunny, who had been living at Dreamwold with Auntie and Father, had become engaged and was married shortly after the birth of the twins. She and her young husband then left for the Orient. I found myself with Auntie in charge of Dreamwold—a housekeeper for my father.

Time passed quickly, summer merging into fall. Father's health seemed good, and he greatly enjoyed playing with the children, Tommy, Harry, and little Dorothy.

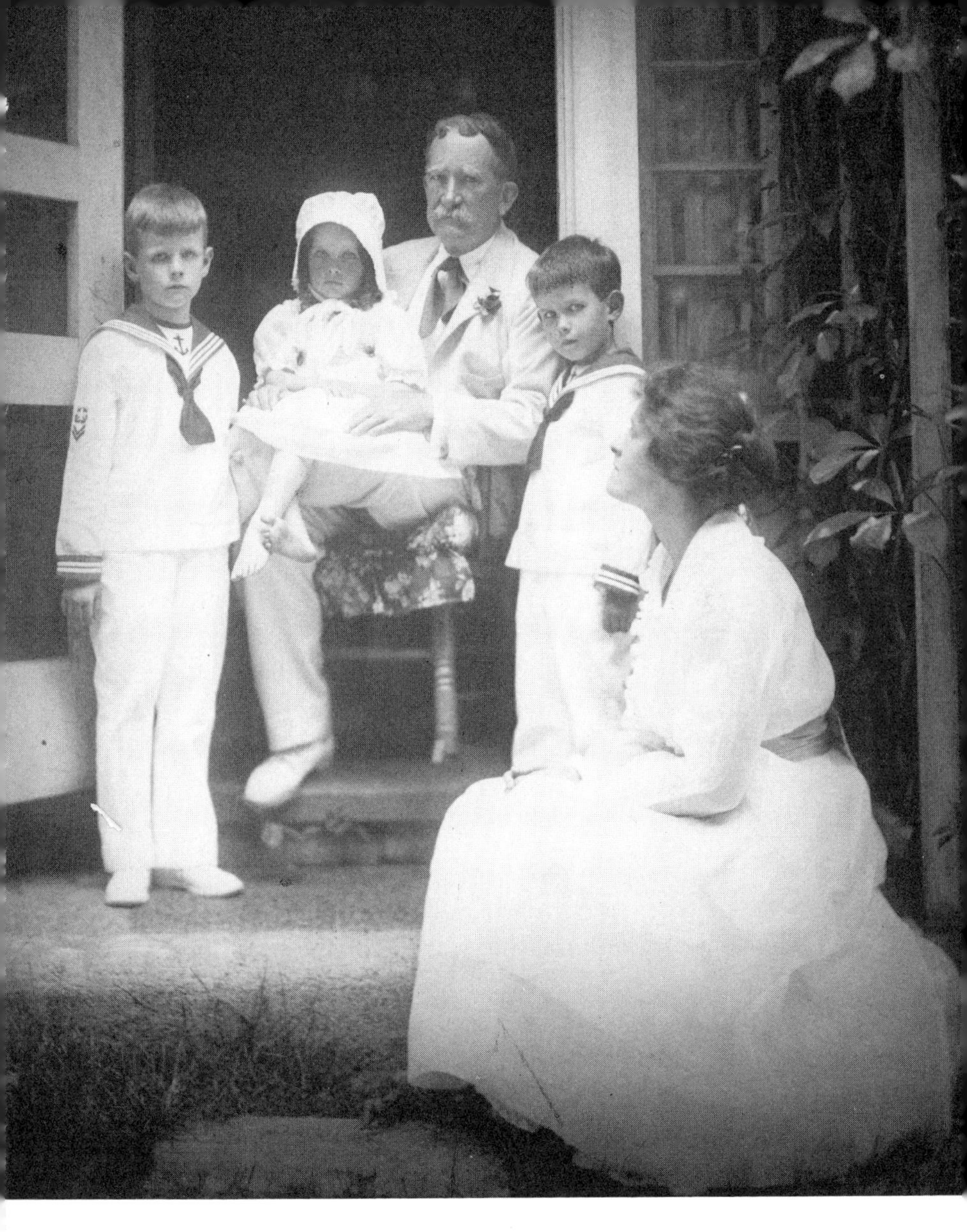

The Copper King in doorway of The Nest at Dreamwold, with grand-children, Harry, Bebs, and Tom; and daughter, Dorothy.

"Here, at The Nest, Father did most of his writing."

The McCalls of Oregon are gathered in front of the living-room fireplace at the family ranch in Central Oregon. The occasion was Mrs. McCall's eighty-second birthday, October 11, 1970. Preparations were under way for the annual pheasant-shoot dinner, celebrating the event. From left: the twins, Sam McCall and Jean (McCall) Babson; Harry McCall; Dorothy, mother of the flock; Governor Tom McCall, and Bebs (McCall) Chamberlain.

Hal planned to be with us during Thanksgiving, Christmas, and on through the New Year holidays.

Suddenly Father's health took a turn for the worse, and during Hal's visit a project was discussed by Father, Doug, and Hal. It was suggested that Hal bring his now-famous registered Holstein dairy cows back to Dreamwold. Cow barns and silos were empty there, as well as most of the fine buildings. Father had gradually been disposing of his own superb stock.

At the time of the discussion, Hal had given up his less-hardy Jerseys for the more sturdy Holstein-Friesens from Wisconsin. Also, after World War I, when beef went to ten cents on the dollar, he had been unable to maintain his beef herd. Stocking Dreamwold's dairy barns with the famous McCall registered Holsteins seemed wise to Father and Douglas but not to Hal, who remained adamant. He would not give up the ranch, so the plan fell through.

Soon Hal returned to the ranch while I stayed on at Dreamwold. For the following year or two Hal returned every two or three months for a six-weeks' stay. As the months went by, with his frequent visits back and forth, I found myself torn between my father and my husband. The split situation of the family could not go on indefinitely. We all realized this—Hal, Father, and myself. Then one day, on what was to become Hal's final visit, Hal called me onto the porch and spoke very seriously,

Farewell to Dreamwold

"Father, then sixty-five, with the twins, Sam and Jean, at Dreamwold —the last time I saw Father alive."

"You have been my girl all my life, Dote, and I love you, but I tell you today that I am not going to live alone any longer!" Dumbfounded, I rushed up to find Father.

"Oh, Pa," I cried, "I have to take the children and go back to the ranch!" Father looked straight at me and said,

"Oh, don't talk nonsense." But when I told him what Hal had said, he answered,

"Pack up your things, Dorothy, and take the children back to the ranch with Hal."

My father was basically a wise man. He was very fond of Hal and they were great pals, but he realized the quiet depth of Hal's feelings. Above all else, Father wanted the Hal McCall family to stay together.

It was a sad day at Dreamwold when we said goodbye to "Granddaddy." Everyone was practically in tears, even the children. I shall always remember Father as I saw him that day. He stood at the front door flanked by the household staff, three maids on one side and the kitchen staff on the other, all faithful retainers down through the years.

Earlier that morning, I had ridden over to the beach on my little bay mare which Father had kept in the stables for me. The tide was low on the beach as I rode up and down at the edge of the ocean. Tears splashed on the horse's neck and bridle, for I felt that this was the end of an era. I would never see my father or Dreamwold again!

14

"To Pa, from whom all blessings flow!"

It was a sad trip back west for Hal and me as we both felt that my father's condition was worsening. From the time we reached the ranch, telegrams—long night letters—started arriving for the children from "Granddaddy." Even with my aunt in residence, Father was a lonely man.

Strangely enough, his illness had been triggered by an automobile accident. . . . My father-in-law, Samuel Walker McCall, who had now completed two years as governor of Massachusetts, 1916-1918, had already served in the United States Congress as representative from Middlesex County, Massachusetts, for twenty years, 1893-1913. In the latter year, 1913, he ran for the

United States Senate, a staunch Republican. When an old friend—a long-time United States Senator—retired, it had been fairly well understood that Samuel McCall would succeed him.

With the senatorial campaign in full swing, my father said to Hal's father,

"Do you think you might have a younger opponent popping up at any time, Sam, and if so, is he a member of a State-Street firm we both know?"

Mr. McCall only laughed, not taking him seriously. Father went on to say, "I know these State-Street boys, Sam, better than you do. Why not let me help you out with this campaign?"

My Lincolnesque father-in-law answered, "Thank you, Tom, and I appreciate your offer, but I've never even given a man a cigar to influence a vote!" He had always had tremendous admiration for the straightforward integrity of Lincoln and in many ways resembled the latter in character and conduct. It is interesting to note that he promoted the building of the Lincoln Memorial in Washington, D. C.

The story of his campaign was written up in newspapers across the nation with special emphasis in the East. The outcome was decided by a two-thirds vote. Meeting after meeting deadlocked in the Statehouse on Beacon Hill. Rumor had it that State-Street money finally bought the deciding vote from Middlesex County.

Glaring headlines flooded the newsstands after McCall's defeat at the Massachusetts Republican Convention.

My father-in-law had remained true to his guiding principles; he had turned down Father's proffered help; but State-Street money had won. Enraged, Father jumped into the gap with an announcement that he would run for the United States Senate.

Years before, Mother had said to Aunt Mary, after one of her heart attacks,

"If one of these should take me off some day, Mary, I hope you will always stay with your brother. I must warn you—try to keep him away from politics. Politics is something he knows absolutely nothing about, even with his long and varied career."

Mother's words proved true. In addition to his lack of political success, it was while campaigning that Father was in the automobile accident that broke five ribs and his collarbone.

Two of my sisters carried on the campaign. Bunny drove the car and Marion did the talking. This spectacular and unusual political campaign resulted in a Republican defeat. A Democrat was elected to the United States Senate.

While he was in the hospital after the unsuccessful race, it was discovered that Father's automobile accident had brought on acute neuritis. This eventually went into diabetes. Throughout his illness his most stalwart friend was John P. Feeney. Finally, after consultation with Mr.

Feeney, it was decided that Dreamwold must go and Father would move to smaller quarters.

His apartment in the Fenway, in Boston, was more than adequate for his needs. With his faithful chauffeur, Joe, he was able to go out for drives in the Park. Feeney would drive with Father on some of these trips and there was always Mary. One day Auntie said to Mr. Feeney,

"I want to tell you how good you have been to my brother." Mr. Feeney answered,

"Miss Lawson, no matter how much I have done for your brother, I could never repay him for what he has done for me."

In those last days, Father had another close friend. It was a strange affiliation. When we first moved into Boston from Winchester, one of the loveliest young women there—famous not only for her beauty but also for her skill in outdoor activities—was Eleonora R. Sears. Eleo was wonderful.

Father's friendship for her was triggered by an incident which had happened on a summer afternoon years before, when the *Dreamer* was coming out of Boston Harbor on her way down the South Shore to Cohasset. Father was relaxing on the afterdeck. It was his custom, through the hot weather, to go back to Cohasset from his office by boat rather than by train.

Suddenly he felt a tremendous jolt as Captain Silva, on the bridge, swung *Dreamer* from her course. Dashing to the rail, he was just in time to see a small sailing boat cut across *Dreamer's* bow. From her skipper, a blue-eyed, golden-haired girl, came a cheery call,

"Hi, Tom. How's copper?"

From Father came an irate shout,

"Fine, Eleo. How's brass?"

This little story probably originated in a newspaper reporter's mind but it was to be told around Boston for years. Father and Eleo Sears eventually became fast friends, friends until the day he died. And it was Eleo who came to see him so faithfully in the Fenway apartment. On his lowest days, he would immediately brighten when he heard Eleo's cheery call and her step on the stair.

Right up until the end, she was still assuring him, "One of these days I'll be riding over and bringing a horse for you too. We'll ride together in the park."

With the beginning of Dreamwold, Father had started an unusual collection of elephants. On the mantel over the living-room fireplace, elephants marched—small ones from the corners to large ones in the middle. Admirers sent them from far and wide and in all sizes and materials. Metal and stone elephants arrived from as far away as India and China.

I remember one elephant particularly and the hubbub it caused in Father's office the day the telephone message announced its arrival at the Boston railroad station.

"There's a rather unusual and large package here for Mr. Lawson. What in the hell shall we do with this live elephant?" The answer was,

"March it right into the zoo!"

Several months before Father died—on February 8, 1925, at the age of sixty-eight—Eleo Sears, remembering the famous elephant collection, had brought him one from the Rue de la Paix in Paris. This elephant turned out to be the tiniest of all in the collection. It was in a small jewel box and lay an inch in width and height—a little elephant in solid silver!

As the Copper King lay dying, one of his last thoughts was for his daughter in the Far West,

"Mary," he whispered to his sister, "I'm in great pain and know I cannot last much longer, but I do wish I could be sure the ranch doesn't prove to be a white elephant around that girl's neck!"

If only Father could have realized that this "elephant," this "Ranch Under the Rimrock," would turn out to be the most productive and enduring of all his achievements.

As long as Father was in the Fenway apartment, cheery night letters continued to arrive for the children. Probably the reason Hal and I could not visualize Father's grave condition was the consistent lightheartedness of these messages.

Then one morning, before daylight, we were awakened by a thumping on the back door, followed by loud calls,

"Mr. McCall, Mr. McCall, I've got a telegram!"

Hal jumped from bed and dashed downstairs to the back door. I also got up, and turning to one of the north windows, stood there in my nightgown. Somehow I knew, without being told, the tragic news. I remained there until I felt Hal's hand on my shoulder. Dry-eyed and almost speechless, I raised my right arm and pointing to the sky over the towering rimrock, I whispered,

"To Pa, from whom all blessings flow. . . ."

In the quiet passing of Thomas W. Lawson, the Copper King, there passed also his fabulous fortune and many of his remarkable achievements. Those that have stood the test of time include Dreamwold at Scituate, Massachusetts, and the western "Ranch Under the Rimrock."[1] However, in the historic little town of Scituate on Cape Code, he has now become legendary; and in faraway Oregon the family of Hal McCall has given new life to the legend.

The final resting place of the Copper King and his beloved wife Jeannie is in Fairview Cemetery at Scituate. A five-foot pillar of white granite bears the name "Lawson." Above is a simple relief carving of a winged horse and his rider contained within an oval, along with

[1] See *Ranch Under the Rimrock* by Dorothy Lawson McCall.

the word, "Dreamwold." Two chairs carved from granite flank the shaft; one reads, "JEANNIE A. LAWSON, Sept. 6, 1857 – August 5, 1906"; the other, "THOMAS W. LAWSON, Feb. 26, 1857–February 8, 1925."

The emblem of Dreamwold–"Pegasus," the winged horse of the Muses, fitting symbol for Thomas Lawson, lover of horses and of poetry.

From Cape Cod